# THE SILENT SCREAM

# THE SILENT SCREAM

Betty Sullivan La Pierre

ISBN 1-59109-208-6

# THE SILENT SCREAM

*To my Mom & Dad, who encouraged me to follow my dreams. I dedicate this book to you with all my love. Acknowledgements Page: I'm infinitely grateful to my critique group, Leila Anne Pina, Selma Rubler and Robert Warren for their undying support in my writing of this novel. Their editing and critique helped to make it all possible. I thank them from the bottom of my heart. Also, I want to thank the Jane Brooks College School for the Deaf in Oklahoma for the invaluable training it gave to me on understanding the deaf. The undaunted love shown for those many children will remain in my heart forever.*

# CHAPTER ONE

*Richard bounced across the rough field on his motorcycle toward* home. He peered in the direction of the front door and wondered why his mother hadn't poked her head out and waved as she usually did when he arrived. She must be busy over the stove, he thought, wheeling into the barn yard.

He jumped off the bike and glanced up at the roof of the house. No smoke curled out of the pipe vent connected to the wood burning stove. That worried him.

Quickly pushing the bike into the barn, he dusted off his jeans and hurried toward the back door. Sniffing the air, he thought it odd that he couldn't smell any food cooking. Mom always had something going on the stove that made his mouth water.

His dog Ruffy hadn't run to greet him either. As he raced up the rickety wooden steps, he glanced quickly under the raised back porch for his large Golden Retriever, but didn't see him. Giving his seat one more dusting, he opened the squeaky screen.

Richard had no more stepped into the kitchen than he staggered backwards against the door jam. He sucked in his breath as he stared in horror at his mother's body sprawled on the floor in a pool of blood. And Ruffy's furry body lay beside her, blood still flowing from the slit in his throat.

He swallowed hard, then forced himself forward, stretching out his arm so that only the tips of his trembling fingers touched his mother's cold, lifeless body. As the smell of death invaded his nostrils, the taste of bile bubbled into his throat

Richard clutched his stomach and stumbled back outside where he leaned over the wooden railing and vomited until his insides ached from the dry heaves. Tears blurred his vision and sobs wracked his whole being. Who would do this horrible thing to his beautiful mother and gentle dog?

He took a deep breath and turned back toward the entry. Maybe what he'd seen was no more than a horrible figment of his imagination. He eased open the door, shot a quick look inside, then slammed it shut. His breath came in ragged spurts as he leaned his forehead against the hard wood. No, dear God. . .it really had happened. His mother and dog were motionless..

Fear slithered down his spine. Could the killer still be in the area? He whirled around and scanned the grounds. Having just come from the empty barn, he glanced toward the chicken coop. The hens were scampering about and pecking the ground as if nothing had happened. He chewed on his lip as a chill rippled through his body.

His first thought was to take his gun and search the countryside until he found the murderer. He started to go inside, but stopped in his tracks. The idea of having to step over his mother's body to get to his room made him shiver. Instead, he stumbled down the steps and ran to the side door. Even though it was locked, he yanked and pulled on the knob, grunting loudly as the tears flowed down his cheeks. Adrenalin surged through his veins as he dashed around the corner of the house to his room's window. He grabbed the screen and ripped it off with his bare hands. Fortunately, the window was open a crack. He wedged his fingers under the rotting wood, heaved it upward and climbed inside.

Leaping to his feet, he stared through the open door of his room which faced the kitchen. The sight of his mother's long black hair flowing across the wooden floor made him feel weak. He quickly shut the door and stood for several minutes, his head resting against the unyielding wood. Hot tears dropped onto his hands.

His eyes squeezed shut, he whipped around and leaned his back against the door. Within a few minutes, he rubbed his sleeve across his nose and took several deep breaths before snatching his twenty-two from the closet. He rummaged in his dresser drawer for a box of shells. How he wished he still had his dad's shotgun. But before his dad had died, he'd insisted that Uncle Joe take that gun along with a couple of others for safe keeping until Richard turned eighteen.

He doubted he'd ever see those weapons again since Uncle Joe had gone back to the Midwest and taken everything with him, including the guns. No one had heard from him since. Of course, dad couldn't have foreseen this horrible incident and what his son would have to face alone. But Richard sure as hell wished Uncle Joe was here now.

Before hunting for the killer, he needed help. The only people he knew well were the Zankers. Richard's family didn't have a phone, so he'd have to ride his motorcycle. The Zanker's ranch started at the bottom of the hill and extended for miles in every direction. Their ranch house was located at the far end, which must be at least ten miles away. There were no two ways about it. He had to go, regardless of how far he had to ride. Grabbing his jacket and clipping the shoulder strap to his gun, he hurried to the barn where he filled the motorcycle with gas. He snapped the gun strap across his chest and over one shoulder so that the twenty-two fit snugly against his back. Throwing his leg over the seat, he started the motorcycle and headed out. Instead of traveling across the pasture, he drove straight for the road, silently praying.

Richard rode for what seemed like hours. Even though the night air seemed cool, he felt hot and feverish. When he finally turned up the long winding road leading to the Zanker's ranch, his heart plummeted. There were no visible lights inside the house. He dashed up the steps to the large front porch and pounded on the door, but received no answer. Not even the dogs raced around the house to greet him. He stood for a moment searching the property for any signs of life. They must have left on a trip, taking their German shepherds with them.

Then a wave of fear surged through him. Had they suffered the same fate as his mother and dog? He frantically tried to see in the windows at the front, but they were all covered with heavy drapes to block out the sun. Racing around to the back side of the house, he looked in every uncurtained window on the way and saw nothing out of the ordinary. When he reached the back door and could see through the large window to the kitchen, he breathed a sigh of relief that everything appeared clean and spotless. He returned to the front yard with a heavy heart. No one here to help. Who could he get? He didn't know anyone in the Copco Lake area, only the boy he'd biked with on occasion up in the hills. He didn't even know his name, much less where he lived. There were no homes to his knowledge between his house and the Zankers. Klamath Falls would be too far to ride tonight. He felt frustrated and confused, unsure of what to do.

Richard gave a reluctant look at the Zanker house and climbed back on his cycle. He made a wide U-turn in the driveway and rode toward home. When he finally reached the road to his house, he cut across the field to the barn, then suddenly, he remembered the lone man who lived in that one room shanty up the road. He made a sharp turn and sped up the hill. But, to his dismay, he found the house dark and deserted. He'd have to try to get help early in the morning. Maybe he'd even find someone on the road. By the time he finally got back to his house and parked the bike in the barn, the moon shone high in the sky. He closed the big wooden door and walked slowly toward the house.

Hesitantly, he pulled open the side door that he'd unlocked and stepped into the hall that led to his room. The foul odor of blood bit into his nostrils. Sweat beaded his forehead and upper lip. He entered his room, sat down on the bed and studied the closed door leading into the kitchen. Placing the gun across his lap, he stared through the window at the moon shadowed yard.

Several hours later, Richard awakened with a start. The twenty-two still clutched in his hand, he slid quietly off the bed and dropped to his knees. The wooden floor beneath him quivered slightly, as if an animal had run across the planks.

He jumped to his feet and flung open the kitchen door. Letting out a cry like a wounded animal, he aimed his gun, shot repeatedly and found he'd killed three rats trying to make a meal of his mother and dog.

He also noticed the sun's rays beginning to filter through the kitchen window, exposing blow flies buzzing the room. Knowing the bodies of his mother and dog couldn't stay in the kitchen any longer, he shrugged on his jacket and headed for the barn. He had to bury them now.

Leaning his gun in the corner, he dragged a shovel and pick to the small creek that ran near the house. Richard's mom had a special old oak tree where she loved to sit with Ruffy when she had time. Richard enjoyed seeing the pleasure on her face as she watched the birds flit from branch to branch. She'd hug the dog close to her with one hand while letting the other dangle in the water trickling along the small stream bed. A picture he'd now hold forever in his heart.

Richard eyed his mother's favorite tree. Dragging the shovel loosely in his hand, he walked around the trunk and studied the ground. Finally, he decided on a spot that stayed shady most of the day, but had a good view of the house and stream. Gripping the spade, he dug into the rock embedded ground. It took him half a day to dig a hole deep enough, as he had to use the pick to remove many small stones and lift or roll the larger ones out of the way. Finally, he laid the shovel aside and wiped his hands down his jeans. He stood for a moment staring down into the hole then up at the small building he'd always called home. The thought of what he had to do made him shudder. His life would never be the same.

Taking a deep breath to build up his courage, he started toward the house. The one thing he hadn't prepared himself for when he stepped into the kitchen was the odor. He gagged and ran back outside, shutting the door behind him.

Rubbing his hands over his face, he sat down on a large boulder in the middle of the yard. Clutching his stomach, he wondered how he could stand that horrible smell. But he had to. Otherwise, it would only get worse. Pulling a bandana from his pocket and tying it around his nose and mouth, he prepared himself to face this horrible ordeal.

The swarming flies were thick and he waved his hands to shoo them away. Holding his breath, he quickly picked up Ruffy's body and carried it outside toward the stream. His arms trembled as he gently placed the dog in the hole. Covering the blood stained tangled fur with a layer of soil so the flies couldn't reach the animal's flesh, he stepped away from the grave and inhaled deeply. Then he glanced toward the house with dread. The next job would be the hardest thing he'd ever attempted in his life.

Back in the kitchen, his insides rolled and jerked as he gathered strength to touch his mother's body. He needed to know how she died, so that when he found the scum who did this, he could give him the same treatment.

Filling a basin of water, he took a clean washcloth and a large towel from the small stash of linens. Nervously, he moved toward her and glanced at the lower half of her body. Her dress had been ripped up to the waist, revealing bloody thighs and her panties were wrapped around her ankles. She'd been brutally raped. His mouth went dry as he covered her nakedness with the towel, then he tenderly closed her eyes.

Tears flowed down his cheeks as he began washing the blood from her face. What would he do without her? He'd lost his dad only the year before and now her. The only human beings that ever understood his problem were now gone. They'd taught him how to read, write and do math and shown him a world of happiness. Even though they were poor, they never lacked for love and laughter. He clutched her small body to his chest. Rocking back and forth, he swore that whoever did this to her would pay the price at the hand of Richard Clifford.

After a tedious half hour of carefully cleaning her face, hair and the jagged cut across her throat, he felt he'd done the best he could. He went to her closet and took out her favorite dress, the one that made her blue eyes stand out like jewels. He recalled how pretty she'd looked two years ago when they attended the town's fair. She'd whirled around the living room, making the skirt swirl out, showing her pretty lace slip. Dad had caught her in his arms, planted a big kiss on her lips, right there in front of him, and told her of her beauty and how much he loved her. Richard would never forget that moment, one of the happiest days of his life.

Struggling for several minutes, Richard finally got the blood soaked dress off her limp body and slid on the clean one. He held her in his arms for a few more moments, kissing her forehead, while his tears mingled with her beautiful long black hair. He lifted the small slender body onto her favorite quilt he'd taken off her bed. She'd like that. Her mother had sewn the wedding ring design for her and dad as a wedding present. Wrapping it neatly around her, he then slowly rolled her into a large plastic tablecloth, safety pinning the ends in hopes it would add some protection from insects.

Cradling her body in his arms, he staggered to the barn. He

knew the police would have to take specimens to help find the murderer, so he couldn't bury her in the ground. He'd purposely didn't clean below her neck, afraid he might destroy evidence. But his heart pulsed with anger every time he thought about leaving such filth on her body.

Richard stood in front of the grain bin which they never used. This would have to do. He gently slid her body inside and secured the lid. At least no rats would get to her now. Composing himself, he went back to the hole where he'd placed Ruffy and finished filling the grave with dirt. He fashioned a cross of small stones on top and patted them into the soil. Shoulders drooping, he stumbled back toward the house and leaned the pick and shovel against the porch.

The realization hit Richard like a bolt of lightening. He would now be the one responsible for what lived and died on this little plot of ground. At that moment, his emotions just seemed to click off.

He threw out some chicken feed and soon the hens were pecking at the ground close to his heels. Watching them scratch and eat, he thought how fortunate he'd been that no varmint had devoured them last night, because he'd forgotten to close up their coop.

Glancing up, he spotted Old Betsy the cow near the pasture gate, her neck stretched over the fence, looking straight at him with her mouth wide open, obviously bawling because she needed milking. Whitey the horse, stood next to her, moving his head up and down. Immediately, Richard went to the cow and led her into the barn. The odor of the decomposing body hadn't penetrated the enclosure so much that he couldn't go ahead and milk her inside. After relieving the cow's misery, he fed the horse and took special effort in finishing up the remaining chores.

When he stepped into the kitchen, he had to put his handkerchief back around his nose and mouth. His first job would be to get rid of that horrible pungent odor. He stoked the stove, then filled a large kettle with water and placed it on the top. While it heated, he searched the cabinets for the big bottle of ammonia he'd seen his mother use for cleaning. Soon, he found it and added a cupful of the strong cleaner to the hot water, then he set to scrubbing the kitchen floor. Working as though in a trance, he rubbed each spot, obsessed with the idea that getting rid of any trace of blood would erase the tragedy. But a deep bitterness gripped his heart and he vowed that he'd find the son-of-a-bitch who did this horrible deed.

After an hour, he leaned back on his haunches and studied the room, trying to picture in his mind what had happened. Had his mother fought the intruder? The blood splattered walls indicated to him that she had. Also, he'd noticed what looked like flesh and blood under her fingernails. If he was right, she'd left her mark somewhere on the body of the murderer that he wouldn't soon forget. Even though Ruffy had always been a gentle animal, he believed the dog had tried to protect his mother, and that's what had gotten him killed.

Richard continued to scour the kitchen until he could see no more stains. He opened the windows and doors for air, then dumped the water far from the house and threw the cloth into the barrel where they burned the trash. Giving the wet kitchen floor time to dry, he ambled toward the front of the house and stood on the edge of what used to be their driveway. Odd, he thought, studying tire tracks that circled the area. Those definitely didn't come from a two wheeler. And as far as he recalled, no one had visited them for a week or more. So someone had been there while he was on his ride. Who, and what did they want?

He decided to take a deeper look in hopes of finding other clues. Searching around the edges of the bushes, he discovered an empty, but fairly new whiskey bottle. No one in his household drank, and people usually weren't so brazen as to toss an empty whiskey bottle into someone's front yard bushes. That is, unless it happened to be the murderer. He started to pick up the bottle, but yanked his hand back when he thought of the possibility of fingerprints. Having read about detectives and police enough to know something about their procedures, he ran into the house and hunted for a clean paper bag. Dashing back outside, he found a long thin stick, inserted it into the neck opening of the bottle, lifted it out of the hedge and dropped it into the container. Carefully carrying it back inside, he put a twister around the top of the sack and stashed it in one of the lower kitchen cabinets.

Returning to the front yard, he searched carefully in hopes of finding other clues. He checked every bush, corner and crevice, while wondering if his mother knew her killer.

Assuming the murderer was a man, Richard frowned and clinched his fist. His father had explained rape to him a couple of years ago and he'd read about such cases in the police magazines. A lump formed in his throat, just thinking about what his mother must have endured. He let out a wail that made the birds fly from the trees in terror.

He picked up a stone and heaved it as far as he could...then another and another...he kept sailing them through the air until his arm ached. Finally, he stopped, dropped his hands on his thighs and sobbed.

Soon, he threw back his shoulders and decided right then and there, the time had come for him to stop crying and act like a man. He had things to do.

# CHAPTER TWO

*Richard rode his motorcycle to the Zankers' place three times* within the next forty-eight hours, but found no one home. Returning from the last run, he continued up the hill before turning into his place in hopes of finding Jerome. His mother had never mentioned the man's last name, so all he knew was, "Jerome, the 'hermit on the hill'". The hermit's personal hygiene made Richard shudder. The man sported long greasy dark hair tucked under a dirty leather hat and a beard spattered with food that flowed down his chest to the top of his belt buckle. And on top of his dirty clothes, he always wore a long flapping navy blue overcoat that looked like it came out of the Civil War. His whole wardrobe reeked. But the thing that bothered Richard the most were those steel blue eyes that peered out from under the floppy brim of his hat. They seemed to stare into his very soul.

During the illness of Richard's dad, Jerome had made several trips to the Clifford's home, bearing gifts of fruit from his trees and vegetables from the produce markets in town. He continued this ritual after Mr. Clifford's death, which Richard concluded as an attraction toward his mother, Francine. But she never returned his attention, so Jerome's trips eventually tapered off. Despite this, Richard figured he could count on the hermit's help, if he could ever find the man home.

He noticed the gas gauge on his cycle had gotten dangerously low. The only gas left had been stored in the barn, which he'd avoided since the smell of his mother's body had permeated the area to the point of unbearable. He'd even started milking Betsy outside.

Today, he covered his nose with a bandana and quickly moved the last gas container under a lean-to built alongside the barn. If he didn't get a refill soon, he'd have to resort to riding Whitey to check on the Zankers, which would take twice as long. Also, if they didn't return within a day or two, he'd have to find help from strangers. His mother's body had deteriorated badly.

Richard remembered about a week before his mother's death that Mr. Zanker had brought over several boxes of supplies, including an extra can of gas. He didn't pay much attention, as the man spoke only to his mother, not to him. Now he wished he'd been more attentive. Zanker might have mentioned his date of return.

Staying busy, Richard tried not to think about his mother's body in the grain bin. Those thoughts made him feel awful. He tried to remember his actions for those first forty-eight hours after finding her and his dog, but couldn't recall anything. He surmised he'd suffered some sort of shock.

Laboring with the chores he'd seen his mom do, he now knew why she always seemed so tired at night. The work never ended. Just keeping the bugs and birds off the plants in the garden took much of his time. He fashioned a scarecrow by nailing two sticks together and hammering it into the ground at one end of the field. He then draped one of her dresses over the crossed sticks and stuck a sun bonnet on the top. When the material flapped in the breeze, it did the trick and kept the birds at bay. Then the bugs took over, so he herded the chickens into the area to eat them. The scarecrow didn't seem to bother them. But the morning he discovered the gophers, he wanted to cry. He stood vigil over the garden with his twenty-two and after a couple of well-placed shots, the varmints' intrusion slowed. It made him wonder how she ever got anything harvested. Yet, every year they had fresh vegetables.

The potatoes were doing fine, the fruit trees that lined the property were heavy with green fruit and the blackberry bushes along the creek were loaded. So, at least he could bank on having fresh fruit in a couple of months. He would store the potatoes under the house on the cool side, like his mom always did. But he'd better get the cookbooks out to learn how to can and make jelly. Otherwise, he'd be mighty hungry come fall.

It made him feel strange when these everyday thoughts took over his mind while his mother's brutally murdered body lay in the grain bin. He so wanted to take action, but something in his head just took over, as if his emotions had gone dead. He needed help soon.

Wearily, Richard plodded toward the porch and sat down on the top step. He glanced out over the small plot of land and gave thanks for having a good water well and a septic tank that his dad had installed. At least he had running water and a bathroom in the house.

Then another worry loomed up in his mind. He had no money. Did his mom owe any bills? He'd better plan a trip to the mailbox. Their box stood at the end of the long dirt road, where the pavement ended. He'd ride the horse down and save the precious gas for more important missions. But before anything else, he'd best check her room for any cash she might have stowed away.

He knew she received some sort of check from the Veterans because his dad had served in the Army. Fortunately, the VA had paid for his dad's burial, saving his mom a big expense. But what good would the check do him? He couldn't cash it. He vaguely remembered his mom saying something about if anything ever happened to her, he'd receive the check in his name. Suddenly, Richard felt downcast and lonely. He felt like he'd turned into two people. One minute he wanted to cry and the next he worried about his next step in life. He hoped Mr. Zanker would hurry and get home. He'd know about these things.

Reluctantly, he got up and went inside the house. He didn't like going into his mother's room and hesitated at the door, taking a deep breath before entering. A strange sensation flowed through him when he started searching through the dresser. When his fingers touched her silky underwear, he drew back and closed the drawer. Having been taught to respect people's privacy, he just couldn't do it. Maybe later, when he got used to the idea of her death.

Glancing at his reflection in the only mirror in the house, he saw his mother's face. He had the same fine honed nose and high cheek bones covered with smooth olive skin. The same deep blue eyes and firm determined mouth. His coal black hair hung just to his collar. His mom never let him grow it any longer because she said only girls wore their hair long as a mark of beauty. Boys sweat too much, she used to say while clipping his strands with scissors. You need to keep it clean and short or else it smells. Thinking of her persuasive logic, he smiled at himself in the mirror.

He'd inherited the tall muscular build of his father. He remembered how mom used to scowl at him with her hands on her hips. "You don't need to grow so fast. I want you to stay my little boy as long as possible."

But her scolding didn't help. He kept growing. His large shoulders and arms required bigger shirts. The beard forming on his jaw would have been the envy of any boy his age. And not an ounce of fat protruded from his firm body. However, he'd noticed his mom's smile of pride when she looked up at him and patted his shoulder. "You remind me of your father," she'd say. Then, she'd frown. "But one would think you're closer to twenty than seventeen."

He felt a lump forming in his throat and his eyes stung with welling tears. Shaking the sad thoughts away, he continued his search in the less private areas of her room. On the bedside table he found a few dollars tucked inside the Bible. Then he went through her closet and found more money stuck in a shoe box along with a few trinkets. He held fifteen dollars in his hand. That would do him for now. He stuck the wad of bills in an empty jar and tucked it away in his closet behind a stack of books. Then, he went back outside.

He spent what free time he could muster practicing with his four inch blade Buck knife which he carried in a sheath on his belt. Flipping the knife in the air, he caught it by the tip of the blade and flung it at the target. Bull's-eye!

Uncle Joe had given it to him for Christmas several years ago. Never dreaming he'd have such a use for it, he narrowed his eyes when he thought about meeting his mother's murderer. He made sure the blade stayed sharp as a razor by honing it on a whet stone every night. No killer would ever escape the wrath of Richard Clifford's knife or gun. Not after what had happened to his mother.

Tom Casey, Private Investigator, better known as Hawkman by family and friends, stood outside the aviary on his back porch and made soft cooing noises to the falcon. His wife, Jennifer had surprised him with this beauty two months ago for his birthday. He couldn't have asked for anything better. His first falcon, Pretty Boy, had died of old age several years ago and he missed the companionship something terrible.

Jennifer had searched the internet many hours before she finally found a breeder of falcons in northern Washington state. She'd secretly arranged for the shipping of the bird and met the plane in Medford, claiming she had a meeting with an editor about one of her books. When she returned with the hawk and presented it to Hawkman, it was the first time he could ever remember being speechless.

This beautiful Gryfalcon female stood about two feet tall with a wing span of fifty or more inches. Her coloring ranged between the pure White Gryfalcon and the Black Gryfalcon, making her a shimmering gray, muting to almost white on her breast line. Jennifer had named her Pretty Girl.

For the past sixty days Hawkman had worked on taming the bird and gaining its trust. He felt the time had come to take her out for a hunt. It made him nervous to think that once he released her, she could fly away forever. But, that was the chance he had to take. The whole joy of owning a falcon was not only the hunt, but the bird returning to sit regally upon your arm.

Jennifer planned to accompany him with her camera. The pictures would enhance the articles she wanted to write for a wildlife adventure magazine. They prepared to spend most of the day, so she packed some sandwiches and sodas for the trip. They'd decided to go high in the hills above the Zanker ranch where there were fewer distractions for the falcon. Hawkman would have to travel over rough terrain in his 4X4 to get to the hill he had in mind.

Summer would soon be here, but the weather today felt like it had already arrived. The sun shone brightly from a cloudless sky, glistening off the new growth and shiny leaves of the trees. Jennifer had her window down, letting the warm air circle her head, whipping her long pony tail about her shoulders. "Pretty Girl looks mighty content sitting on that perch."

"She seemed to take to it from the first day I put her on it," Hawkman said, keeping his gaze ahead as he steered around the rough spots in the field. "I think she likes to ride in the truck."

Jennifer smiled, hanging on to the door handle as they bounced along. Then she pointed out the window at the small house sitting off by itself in the distance. "Wonder who lives there?"

Hawkman squinted into the sun, shading his face with his hand. "Don't know. Could be someone working for one of the ranchers. I'll have to ask Herb Zanker the next time I see him."

They continued for about another half mile before he pulled the truck under a shade tree and parked. Taking the long leather glove from the seat, he slipped it onto his arm and held it in front of the falcon. Pretty Girl immediately climbed aboard.

Jennifer grinned and nodded in approval. "Hey, she did that rather smoothly."

"We've been practicing."

Hawkman slipped the soft leather hood over the hawk's head and strolled several yards away from the truck. Jennifer followed, clicking the camera.

He stopped in the middle of the open area and glanced at her. "You ready? I'm going to remove the hood and I haven't the vaguest idea what she'll do."

Jennifer took a moment to focus the camera, then nodded. "Yes, go ahead."

Gently, he removed the soft leather from the bird's head. Pretty Girl ruffled her feathers, then turned her head toward him, but made no attempt to lift off his arm.

Jennifer laughed. "You've trained her so well to sit there, she doesn't know she's supposed to fly."

Putting his fist on his hip, he grinned. "Well, Pretty Girl, I purposely didn't feed you this morning so that you'd be ready to hunt." He gave an upward jerk to his arm and the falcon flapped her wings. They watched her gain altitude and circle before she pulled out and headed toward a small wooded area to their left.

Jennifer's gaze followed the bird's flight and then she whispered, "Please come back soon, Pretty Girl."

When Hawkman removed the glove and tossed it into the cab of the truck, a movement in the nearby trees caught his eye. He studied the area, but saw nothing and decided it must have been a deer or possibly a bear. Suddenly, a glint of light caught his attention and he frowned. Keeping his voice calm, he motioned for Jennifer. "Come over here behind the truck."

She ambled toward him, a puzzled expression on her face. "Why?"

"There's someone in that stand of trees with a gun."

⚜⚜⚜⚜⚜

The next morning, after Richard finished his normal chores, he proceeded to build a fire under the big black cauldron outside. He had watched his mother do the wash many times and tried to remember the steps he'd seen her take. It took him several minutes to fill the huge vat half full of water. After testing it with his hand, he shook his head. It would take a long time to heat up that batch of cold well water.

He decided he better stoke the fire some more and started for the wood pile when he spotted a dust cloud rising about a half mile away. At first he thought it a dirt devil created by the brisk winds, but after studying the formation, realized it was a truck traveling across the open field. Who would be out this time of the morning? Possibly the killer? He'd read where sometimes they'd go back to visit the crime scene. How sick, he thought.

He turned on his heel, ran across the yard and into the house. Grabbing his loaded gun from the corner of the kitchen, he threw some extra bullets into his pocket then headed back outside. He jogged through the trees, following the course of the vehicle but keeping well inside the shadowed area as he approached the small knoll that jutted out of the ground like a misplaced hill.

When he reached the edge of the trees, the sight surprised him. He didn't expect to see a man, woman and a bird. For a moment, he stood in plain sight before stepping back into the shadows. What were they doing way out here? He watched with fascination as the man walked to the center of the mound with a stately bird resting on his arm. Suddenly, the hawk flew high into the sky. Richard remembered reading about these birds in history books his mother had checked out of the library. They were called falcons. He'd never seen a real one, only in pictures.

Figuring these people weren't killers, he breathed a sigh of relief and sat down on a large boulder to watch. He wondered if they would help him? But his mind closed to his needs as he spotted the bird circling high above the two people. Fascinated, he watched the man put on the long glove and walk back to the center of the knoll. The woman had her camera to her eye.

Richard observed with interest as the big man held his arm high. The bird teasingly circled, swooped down close to the truck, then made a sharp turn and headed up high into the sky. He could see the man's lips moving and wondered what one would say to a bird, but he was too far away.

Something about this big man reminded Richard of his father except his dad didn't have a patch over his eye. Maybe it was his slow methodical movement as he tried to coach the bird down. Yes, that must be it. His dad had shown patience like that while teaching Richard his lessons. It made him want to meet these people and find out where they lived.

The sun had climbed high in the sky and Richard figured he'd better get back to the house and check on the wash water. His fire could have gone out by now. He'd hoped to see the falcon land, but the silly bird kept circling a couple of feet above their heads. Just as he stood to leave, the hawk made another pass, but this time landed gracefully on the man's arm. Richard smiled, feeling the triumph in his own chest.

He sauntered back to the house, his heart growing heavy as he thought about his own mom and dad, but fought the tears that almost blurred his vision. No, he thought, no more crying. It tears me up inside. Straightening, he threw the gun upon his shoulder and marched like a soldier the rest of the way home.

Rubbing his shirts, jeans and underwear on the scrub board in the tub of hot water, like he'd seen his mother do, kept his mind off his sorrows. He then took the clothes to the stream, gave them a final rinse and hung the dripping articles from the rope line strung between two trees.

That evening, he lay in bed and thought about the beautiful bird and the two people he'd seen on the knoll. Had they seen him? What difference did it make if they had? He shouldn't have cowered under the trees. Instead, why hadn't he walked up that hill and introduced himself. They probably would have helped him. Turning over, he pulled the covers over his head. He felt so alone. But he couldn't wait any longer to get help. Tomorrow, he'd have to find someone, stranger or not.

# CHAPTER THREE

*As the truck bounced across the rough field toward the road,* Jennifer eyed Hawkman who seemed preoccupied with private thoughts. "Why so quiet? Pretty Girl did everything right, even though it took her a while to realize you were waiting for her to land on your arm. You've done a good job training that bird."

He jerked his head around as though awakened from a deep slumber. "Huh? Oh yeah, thanks. Sorry, my mind drifted."

"What are you worried about?"

"Can't figure out why that person stayed within the shadows of the trees watching us and didn't come forward. Why would he hide?"

She slumped back against the seat. "Oh, Hawkman, you're suspicious of everyone. Maybe he'd been working in the field and felt his clothes were too dirty. Or, he might have been skeptical about what we were doing out there. We must have looked mighty strange; you with a bird on your arm and me with a camera. These ranch hands aren't use to that type of thing."

"But he had a gun."

"So? Lots of men carry guns up here. This is the time of year rattlers shed their skins. You know how dangerous snakes are when that takes place."

"Yeah, you've got a point. At least he didn't fire at us."

Jennifer rolled her eyes. "Well, if we'd acted half-way friendly, he might have come over and chatted."

He nodded. "You're right. The next time I come up here, I'll make sure I meet him."

"Maybe he lives in that little house we passed. We weren't far from it."

"That's true. I'll be a good neighbor and stop by the place tomorrow."

"You plan on coming back?"

"It's a good spot to train Pretty Girl, and once I start this, I'll need to do it every day until it becomes natural to her."

"I'll pass on coming. I need to get my article written." She held up the digital camera. "By the way, this gift you got me is great. I don't have to wait for the pictures to be developed and have more time for writing."

He smiled. "Glad it's working out." He knew she liked the house quiet so she could concentrate. The timing would be perfect for him to get out and work with the falcon.

⊹⊱⊰⊹⊱⊰⊹⊱⊰⊹

The next day Herb and Elsie Zanker returned from their out-of-state vacation. They'd gone to visit one of their daughters and ended up staying a few days longer than planned. Elsie had the washing machine loaded when Herb came into the laundry room.

"I better run over to the Cliffords' and find out if their supplies held out."

"Good idea." She went into the kitchen and poured flour and sugar from her own canisters into plastic sacks and handed them to Herb. "Give these to Francine. I'm sure she's running low."

He hadn't been gone long before Elsie heard the pick-up return and come to a screeching stop. Herb ran into the house. She dropped the clothes into the laundry basket and met him in the living room. His face pale, he rushed past her and headed straight for the phone. "Francine's been murdered."

Elsie's hands flew to her face as she stopped in her tracks. "Dear God!" Her gaze traveled to the window where she could see Richard's sagging form pacing the porch. She immediately brought him inside.

When Herb finally hung up, Elsie stared at him in disbelief. "What happened?"

He mopped his brow with his handkerchief. "Four days ago, Richard returned from a motorcycle ride and found Francine and the dog with their throats slit on the kitchen floor. He came to our house for help. But after two days, he buried the dog and put Francine's body in the grain bin to protect it from rodents. The barn smells to high heaven."

Elsie's hands again covered her face. "How horrible! Why didn't he try to find other help?"

"The boy's been brought up in isolation and didn't know who else to trust besides us." He pounded his fist on the end of the table. "What a time for us to be gone. I just hope the authorities won't suspect the boy had anything to do with this."

She grabbed his arm and frowned. "Oh Herb, the boy adored his mother and that dog was his faithful companion. He wouldn't have harmed either one."

"You and I know that, but he's a stranger to the rest of the community. Nobody really knew the family. They stayed to themselves because of their affliction."

Elsie glanced at Richard's back as he stared out the window. "I can tell you right now, I'll stick by him," she said, emphatically."

He patted her on the shoulder. "So will I. But I've got to get the boy back to the house so he can show the police where he put the bodies. It's going to be pretty traumatic."

Looking downcast, she twisted the edge of her apron. "That poor child. He's been through enough." She glanced at Herb with moist eyes. "Maybe I should go over with you."

He shook his head. "That won't be necessary. I knew something had happened the minute I walked in the door and saw that boy's face. He's grown into a man within a few short days"

⋯⋯⋯⋯⋯

Expecting to be gone for several hours, Hawkman made a sandwich and tucked it along with a canteen of water into a backpack. He gave Jennifer a peck on the cheek as she concentrated on the computer monitor. Leaving with the falcon on his arm, he'd already decided to stop at the small house on the way to the knoll. It was possible the person who'd watched them lived there.

Instead of cutting across the field in the 4X4 as he'd done yesterday, he continued down to the seldom used logging road and headed for the small hovel. When he drew closer, it surprised him to see two police cars, one being the sheriff's, a coroner's wagon and Herb Zanker's pick-up parked in front. He pulled to the opposite side of the dirt driveway and secured the falcon's tether to the portable perch before getting out.

Not knowing what to expect, Hawkman approached the front door cautiously and had just raised his fist to knock when a handsome young male in his early twenties opened the door. A look of bewilderment registered on the young man's face. He quickly turned away and motioned for Herb Zanker to come forward.

Herb, his face solemn, pushed open the screen. "Glad you're here. I might need your help."

Puzzled by all the mystery, Hawkman lowered his voice. "What's going on? And who's the fellow who opened the door?"

"That's Richard Clifford. His mother's been murdered, along with his dog. He buried the retriever out back, but put his mother's body in the grain bin inside the barn. The coroner has some of the men digging up the dog right now."

Hawkman rubbed his chin. "You've lost me Herb. Did the boy murder his mother?"

Herb threw up both hands. "Oh no! He found them after returning from a motorcycle ride. He tried to reach me, but I've been gone for two weeks. Because of the decomposition of the bodies and rats finding their way into the house, he decided he had to do something with the bodies."

Hawkman stared at him in puzzlement. "I think Richard better fill me in. I can't make heads or tails out of what you're telling me." He glanced over at the boy who stood staring out the front door, his back to him. "Richard, tell me what happened, please."

Herb touched Hawkman's arm. "Oh, I'm sorry. I forgot to tell you the boy's deaf. So was his mother. But he can read your lips quite well. Just make sure he's looking at you. And if you have any problems communicating with him, just write it down. He carries a small pad of paper and pencil at all times."

Hawkman frowned. "You mean he's mute?"

"Not really." Herb shrugged. "He'll talk to most adults. But he told me once that his voice must sound funny, because kids laughed at him. So, he doesn't speak too often."

"Does he sign?"

"No. His mother never allowed it. She figured if he could read lips and use his voice, there would be no need for sign language. Talking to her meant, getting along in today's society."

Taking a deep breath, Hawkman stepped forward and patted Richard's shoulder. The boy whirled around. He put his hand out. "Hello. My name's Tom Casey, but most people call me Hawkman."

A slight smile formed at the corners of Richard's mouth as he shook his hand. "Hawk Man?" he asked, his eyes wide and questioning.

"Yes."

Richard pointed out the window. "You were on that hill yesterday, right?"

Hawkman figured this was the person he'd spotted in the trees. "You saw us?"

Richard nodded. "You have a bird. A falcon?"

"Yes. Would you like to see her?"

The boy's eyes sparkled. "Yeah!"

They started for the door just as a policeman came in the back way. The deputy dashed toward Richard and grabbed his arm, spinning him around roughly. "Where you think you're goin', boy? You ain't leavin' here."

Hawkman reached over and took a firm hold of the officer's wrist and removed it from Richard's body. "There's no need to rough up this boy."

The officer yanked his hand away. "Who the hell are you?"

About that time, Detective Williams followed from outside. "What's going on, Frank?"

"This here dumb mute tried to leave with this one-eyed guy."

Williams shot him a disgusted look, then turned his attention to Hawkman and extended his hand. "Hello, Casey. What brings you out this way?"

"I started up to the knoll to do some bird training when I noticed all the police vehicles. Thought I'd stop to see if I could be of assistance."

Williams scratched his side burn and shook his head. "We've got quite a situation here. The boy claims someone killed his mother and dog several days ago while he was on a motorcycle ride. He buried the dog out back and put his mother's body in the grain bin in the barn to protect her from rats until he could get help. He says he went to Zankers but they weren't home."

Hawkman turned his back toward Richard. "You think the boy's guilty?"

"Hard to say. Of course, all we have to go on is his word."

"If he killed her, why would he hang around for Zanker to get home?" Hawkman asked. "He could have easily run away on that bike and no one would have known the difference for a long time."

The detective shrugged. "Yeah, I thought about that. Doesn't fit, does it? But he's the only suspect we have at the moment."

Frank, the police officer, pointed toward Richard's waist. "Well, you better check that knife he's a totin' on his belt. That could easily be the murder weapon."

Richard's face paled. He stepped back and shook his head vehemently.

Williams shot a stinging glare at the officer. "Let's not jump to any conclusions. We'll wait for the coroner's report." He jerked his thumb toward the door. "I think they could use your help out back."

The disgruntled officer swaggered out.

Hawkman watched him leave, then gave Williams a wary smile. "Where'd he come from? Never seen him before."

"New man, only been on the force a few months. He's a cocky bastard, but in this county we can't be picky. Cops are hard to come by up here."

"I'd like to talk to you about what happened, but not in front of the boy. Want to step out to my truck?"

Williams nodded. "Sure."

They walked around to the far side of the 4X4. "Herb says that boy is a darn good lip reader. I sure don't want him to know what I'm saying."

Williams chuckled as he glanced back toward the house. "I think this will do. We'll just keep our heads turned away from Richard's view."

Hawkman leaned against the fender and folded his arms across his chest. "I couldn't make heads or tails out of Zanker's story. Maybe you can enlighten me."

Williams repeated the details. "If Richard's telling the truth, we don't have much to go on."

Hawkman chewed on a toothpick, studying the detective. "How old is he?"

"Seventeen."

"Oh, man, he looks so much older. Where does he attend school? Bet he's one hell of an athlete."

"Home schooled by his deaf mother."

"How'd she teach him?"

"From what I understand, she taught in a school for the deaf back in Oklahoma before she got married. This particular school didn't believe in sign language, so they taught the students how to speak. You can understand him, even though his voice is monotone."

"Where's his father?" Hawkman asked.

"He died a year ago of cancer."

"Sounds like the boy had had enough tragedy for a life time." He shook his head and glanced toward the house. "Hard to believe these people have lived here for that long and I've never heard of them."

"Obviously, they didn't socialize much. Doesn't appear they have much money. And they may have used the back route to Oregon to get their supplies. No sales tax up there."

Hawkman nodded. "Yeah, makes sense. But where are their wheels to get there?"

"I asked the same thing. Zanker said they had to sell their truck to pay for some of the dad's medications near the end. After the father's death, Herb and his wife have looked after the boy and his mother, making sure they had all the supplies they needed until they got back on their feet."

"Who owns this place?"

"The father bought it four or five years ago. Guess it will go to Richard when he becomes of age. It has a good well and enough acreage for them to have a cow, a horse and a nice garden. The father managed to get the septic tank installed and the water plumbed before he died. So they're pretty self-sufficient. Zanker said the mother didn't have a lazy bone in her body. Took over the chores when her husband became ill and handled everything."

Hawkman's jaw tightened. He took a step away from the truck, hooked his thumbs in his jeans back pockets and gazed over the small plot of land. "Hard to believe people would be satisfied with the bare necessities in this day and age. So why the hell did someone come way up here and destroy their tranquility?"

# CHAPTER FOUR

*Richard's gaze followed the detective and the man with the eye-*patch as they walked down the small slope from the front of the house toward the parked vehicles. He mouthed the name Hawkman several times until he felt it roll smoothly off his tongue. He liked that guy. Maybe one day they'd be friends.

The two men kept their heads averted so Richard couldn't read their lips. It worried him that this stranger might think he killed his mother. How could he convince him that he would never hurt any living thing, especially his own mother and loving dog. But once he found the killer. That would be a different story.

Richard finally turned from the window. "Mr. Zanker, why are they taking so long to dig up Ruffy?"

Herb shook his head. "Don't know, son."

"Should be easy, I dug out all the rocks." He walked to the window that overlooked the back area and watched the coroner sift through each shovel of dirt. Guess they find clues even in the soil, he thought.

When the two men finally lifted Ruffy out of the hole, Richard sucked in his breath. They placed the dog on the stretcher and he observed with curiosity as the coroner measured the animal from head to toe, then wrote everything down on a clip board. Soon, they covered Ruffy with a sheet of plastic and put him into the van. The coroner shifted some papers on his board then he and Sheriff Daniels walked toward the barn. The two attendants hopped into the vehicle and followed.

Richard couldn't see them anymore from where he stood, so he went back to the front window to check on the detective and Hawkman. Within a few minutes, he felt the vibration of the back door slam and glanced around to see the deputy he didn't like, come staggering inside with a handkerchief over his nose. He looked a bit green around the gills, like he might vomit right there on the living room floor.

Mr. Zanker jumped up, grabbed the officer's arm and guided him straight through the house and out the front door where the man disappeared behind one of the trees. He soon reappeared, wiping his face. When Williams and Hawkman noticed the deputy's condition, they hurried toward the house.

A pungent odor drifted through the opened doors and Richard recognized the smell of his mother's body. He figured they'd lifted her out of the grain bin and the coroner was taking measurements like he'd done on the dog. His stomach churned and his heart pounded. He didn't want her taken away. Somehow he'd retained a certain calm knowing she was nearby. He shook off his anxiety, knowing it had to be done. Her remains would hold clues about her murderer. The thought of her being violated made his blood run cold and his hands clenched into fists.

The coroner poked his head in the back door just as the detective and Hawkman entered the front. "I need someone to identify the woman."

Richard read the man's lips and came forward. But Zanker stepped ahead of him and shook his head.

"No, son. I'll do it. You've been through enough."

"It's okay, Mr. Zanker. She's my mom." Richard held his bandana over his nose and headed out the door.

But the boy had no inkling of what a corpse looked like after a few days. Fortunately, the coroner had her zipped into a plastic bag with only her head exposed. But that alone, caught Richard by surprise and he froze. His face turned ashen. If he hadn't recognized her hair and the collar of her dress, he'd have sworn someone exchanged her body for that of some ugly monster.

He backed away, staring at the pouch that contained his

beautiful mother. His stomach knotted and his knees started to buckle. Suddenly, a strong hand gripped his arm and guided him around to the side of the house. Through a flood of tears, he made out the face. "Thank you, Hawkman." Taking a deep breath, he wiped his eyes and neck with the bandana.

"Take it easy. It'll pass. It isn't easy viewing someone you love in that condition."

Richard stepped back around the corner of the house to watch his mother being loaded into the coroner's wagon. As the van drove off, a lump swelled in his throat, causing him great difficulty in breathing. Mr. Zanker, seeing Richard's problem, pulled him toward the porch and sat him down. He went inside and got a glass of water, then plopped down beside the boy and put an arm around his shoulders, giving him a manly hug.

"Son, why don't you come and stay at my house for a few days?"

Richard shook his head. "Thanks, Mr. Zanker. But I have to take care of the garden and animals or everything dies."

Williams and Sheriff Daniels stood off to one side of the porch and couldn't help but overhear Richard's monotone voice as it carried across the air.

Williams shot a look at Daniels. "Do we have to take the boy in to question him? Or can we talk to him here."

"I'd bet my gun that boy's innocent," Daniels said.

"Why's that?" the detective asked.

"When I helped the coroner lift that woman's body from the grain bin, her face, neck and arms had been washed clean of blood. She had on a fresh dress and her body had been wrapped in a homemade quilt. I've never known of a murderer to show such respect. It took a lot of guts for the kid to do that."

"That's true," said Williams. "Let's see if he kept the clothes she had on."

Daniels hooked his thumbs in his back pockets. "Wouldn't blame him if he burned them."

"He appears intelligent and might realize evidence could be present."

The two men approached Herb and Richard. Williams stepped in front with his hands clasped behind his back. "I know this isn't easy, but we need to start the investigation as soon as possible.

Richard, you obviously changed your mother's dress. Did you by any chance keep the clothes she had on when you found her?"

Richard nodded and went inside the house. He returned within seconds, carrying a clear plastic bag that held the blood stained garments and handed it to the detective. "I didn't want her in that dirty dress. Maybe there's some clues on it."

Williams patted the boy's shoulder. "Good thinking." The detective stood for a moment, shifting his feet, then glanced at Richard. "Do you plan on staying here at the house?"

The boy nodded. "I can't leave. The garden and animals would die without me."

⊹⊱⊰⊱⊰⊱⊰⊹

Hawkman stood off to one side, but not out of earshot. He'd already decided to get involved in this case, either through the police department or on his own. The boy needed help.

He'd watched the deputy get sick behind the tree and thought it odd that a man of his status hadn't gotten used to seeing dead bodies. Maybe he'd never seen one in such a decomposed condition. And granted, one never gets used to that smell. He'd watched the deputy's partner rescue him and whisk the ill man away in the black and white.

He waited for Williams and the sheriff to finish their business with Richard before he returned to his truck and pulled on the leather glove. Once Pretty Girl stepped on his arm, he untied the tether, placed the hood on her head and strolled toward the garden area. He felt Richard watching his every move and knew he would follow as soon as everyone left. Sure enough, the cars had barely pulled out onto the road before Richard bounded toward him. He stopped a short distance away, his eyes sparkling in the evening light.

Hawkman smiled. "Are your chickens locked up for the night?"

Richard dashed to the chicken coop, checked inside, closed the wooden door and threw the board latch to lock them in. He raced back and stood a few feet from Hawkman. "They're safe now," he said, in a resonating tone.

The falcon stiffened on Hawkman's arm. "Easy, girl. Everything's okay." He gave her a few seconds to relax, knowing it wouldn't take long for her to get used to that strange voice. When she'd settled down, he glanced at Richard. "Ready to see her take off?"

Richard nodded so enthusiastically that Hawkman suppressed a grin, figuring there'd be a loud snap and the boy's head would drop to the ground.

Slowly, Hawkman removed the hood and tucked it into his pocket, then keeping his actions smooth, he lifted his arm. The falcon gave him a wary look until he jerked his arm upward, then she spread her wings and lifted above his head, flying in circles as she gained altitude.

From the gleam in Richard's eyes, Hawkman knew the boy loved the sight of the bird's graceful flight. Then suddenly, to their amazement, she came spiraling down and headed straight for the garden. In one swoop, she had a gopher in her talons and headed for a nearby stand of trees.

Richard laughed and pointed at the hawk winging away. "The falcon saved my garden."

Hawkman heard the bawling cow and spotted her heading for the barn. He touched Richard's arm and pointed. Acknowledgement flashed across the boy's face and he ran to the house to get his milk bucket. Hawkman grinned to himself. Once the boy got over the shock of the trauma that had occurred, he would have his chores down pat without being reminded.

While waiting for the falcon's return and Richard to finish milking, Hawkman sauntered down near the stream where the dog had been exhumed. The odor had faded, but the hole lay open and exposed. Not good for a boy trying to recover from the brutal deaths of the two he loved most.

He walked back to the garden and Pretty Girl soon returned, landing on his arm as if she'd done it a million times. "You're a smart bird," he said. "Doesn't take you long to catch on."

He placed her inside the truck on her perch, then went back to the burial site near the stream. Picking up a shovel left by the coroner's crew, he began scooping dirt into the large hole. Daylight would soon end, so he hurried, hoping to get it filled before the sun went down. While shoveling, he wondered where Richard's mother would be buried. And he mustn't forget to ask about the dog. The boy would need to know these things for his peace of mind. He knew the law wouldn't permit Richard to bury the animal close to the stream. Maybe Ruffy could be cremated and Richard could scatter the ashes over the land.

He had no idea how long the coroner would need Francine's remains. But he'd make a point to have a talk with him in the next few days. He'd look into the possibility of her being buried next to Richard's father. Or even in the same plot. He'd heard of this before and it might save Richard some expense.

About the time Hawkman thought he'd have to quit because of darkness, the area suddenly lit up. He jerked up his head to see Richard standing with a kerosene lantern and a shovel in his hand. The two men worked together for several more minutes, then they patted down the soil and rolled some of the big rocks onto the fresh dirt, giving the area a more natural appearance.

They walked in silence to the house and leaned the shovels against the side of the porch. Richard held out his hand. "Thanks again, Hawkman."

⟨⋅⟩⊹⟨⋅⟩⊹⟨⋅⟩⊹⟨⋅⟩

Her eyes full of concern, Jennifer met Hawkman and the falcon at the door. "I was getting worried."

"I've got a lot to tell you, but first let me put Pretty Girl to bed. Is there anything to eat?"

"I'll fix you a sandwich."

They sat at the kitchen bar while he ate. Jennifer's hazel eyes wide with interest as he related the events of the day. After he finished, she slapped the counter with her hand. "Darn, I wish I'd gone with you now."

"You'll have plenty of opportunities. That boy needs someone to relate to. About the only friends he has is old man Zanker and his wife, Elsie and they're fine, don't get me wrong. But, he needs someone closer to the age of his folks. We fit the bill."

She frowned. "Are you sure there's no family around?"

"It doesn't appear there is, but I'll check with Zanker tomorrow. I'll run into town first thing in the morning to the livestock store. Richard has a cow, horse and chickens to feed, and I have no idea about his money situation or if he has any at all. Plus, the only vehicle around there is his motorcycle. They had to sell his dad's pick-up to buy medicine for his last days."

"What about his food situation?"

Hawkman shook his head. "I haven't the vaguest idea. I do know he has electricity and running water. And obviously there's a septic tank on the property, because there's an indoor bathroom. Also there's a small refrigerator in the kitchen."

"That settles it. I'm going to town with you. I'll stock his cabinets while you tend to the livestock."

The next day, Hawkman dropped Jennifer at the supermarket while he went to the feed store. Then they headed for Richard's place, leaving the falcon at home.

Hawkman backed up to the gate so he could unload the grain and bales of hay he'd purchased. Richard walked out of the barn carrying a rake, a puzzled expression on his face. Hawkman introduced him to Jennifer, who explained that she'd brought some groceries that needed to be put away. Richard quickly grabbed a couple of the sacks and darted toward the house.

She smiled at Hawkman. "That boy has been raised with manners."

He nodded and opened the gate so he could back into the barn. Jennifer started toward the house with her arms loaded, but Richard met her half way and took the sacks from her. He dropped them on the kitchen table and pointed toward the barn. "I'll go help Hawkman now."

⟨⊹⟩⊱⟨⊹⟩⊱⟨⊹⟩⊱⟨⊹⟩

Jennifer waved him out and began putting the perishables into the refrigerator. Opening one of the cabinet doors, she noticed the shelves were almost bare. Thank goodness she'd remembered how their son Sam wanted plenty of 'warm-up and eat' canned goods, along with all kinds of sandwich makings, including peanut butter.

She busied herself stocking the shelves and had just emptied one of the sacks when she heard a vehicle pull up outside and glanced out the window. She frowned at the police car, wondering what they wanted. Before she could fold the sack in her hand, a loud knocking echoed throughout the house. She hurried to the door.

"Yes?"

The big man standing on the porch looked surprised. "Oh! Excuse me, ma'm. But I'm lookin' for Richard Clifford. Hope he ain't left the country."

Jennifer felt an immediate dislike for the officer. His sarcasm grated her nerves. She put her hands on her hips. "Of course not. Why do you say such a thing?"

"Just checkin' to see if that little murderer is still around."

"I beg your pardon." Jennifer narrowed her eyes and threw back her shoulders. "Please leave these premises at once!"

The officer glanced back at his partner standing behind him. "Oh, Jim, we got a feisty one on our hands today." Just as he put his hand on the screen handle, Hawkman walked up behind her.

# CHAPTER FIVE

*Hawkman rested his hands on Jennifer's shoulders as Richard hung* back and watched.

"What's the problem, hon?"

"This your woman?" the deputy asked.

"Yes, she's my wife. If that's any of your business."

Frank Alberts took his hand off the screen handle and stepped back. "No, sir. None of my business."

"What brought you way out here?" Hawkman asked.

"Just checkin' on the boy. Seein' if everything's okay."

Jennifer's eyes narrowed and she put her hands on her hips. "That's not what you said."

"Now, ma'm, I didn't mean no harm."

"Who sent you out here to check on Richard?" Hawkman asked.

"No one. Just happened to be out in this neck of the woods and thought I'd come by."

"I see. What's your role in this investigation?"

Alberts stepped back and raised a hand. "Now, don't get on your high horse. I'm on my way."

Hawkman and Jennifer strolled out on the porch and watched the patrol car drive down the road.

Jennifer frowned. "I don't like that man. He's crude and doesn't even act like a policeman. His partner didn't say a word, just stood there and fidgeted."

Hawkman put an arm around her shoulders as they went back inside. Rubbing his chin thoughtfully, he glanced at her. "Think I'll talk to Williams about Albert's interest in this case."

Meanwhile, Richard strolled over to the window, then turned toward them, his thumbs hooked in his front jeans pockets. "I don't like that policeman. He's not honest."

Jennifer studied his face. "Why do you say that?"

"Mom said it's all in the eyes. His jump all around when he's talking. He never looks at you. He's hiding something."

Hawkman reached over and patted his shoulder. "We shouldn't make a judgment until we have facts. The deputy might be genuinely interested in your well being. He just shows it differently."

Richard shook his head. "You can't hide lies. Mom always knew when I told a fib by just looking into my eyes."

Jennifer smiled. "Your mother was a wise woman. It takes years to learn how to read facial expressions."

The boy's gaze scanned the floor. "I could tell my mom died scared."

Jennifer shot a look at Hawkman, then changed the subject. She touched Richard's arm. "Come into the kitchen and show me where you'd like to store the canned goods."

Hawkman left them sorting groceries and went to the barn. The building had pretty much aired out and he finished stacking the grain bags against the inside wall. He then drove the truck around to the front of the house and parked under a big shade tree. Reaching under the seat, he pulled out the cell phone. It made him uncomfortable that Richard was deaf and alone in this desolate area. The unexpected visit from the deputy enhanced the feeling. If he could figure out a way for the boy to use this instrument, he'd feel a lot better. The emergency 911 wouldn't be a problem. But what if he wanted to reach me, how could he do it?

Hawkman turned it over in his hands several times, then dialed his house. He put the phone against his ear and closed his eyes, trying to put the external sounds out of his mind. But it wasn't easy to block out the leaves rustling in the wind and the buzzing of the phone. He concentrated harder, focusing on his other senses.

Soon, he could feel the vibration of the ringing against his head He counted slowly and at the count of six, the tone stopped. Then the answering machine came on. At the count of ten, the beep sounded. So, on the count of eleven Richard could be instructed to give a message and it wouldn't make any difference whether the phone had been answered or not. The party on the receiving end would hear him. Hawkman liked the idea and bounded out of the truck, then stopped short. Richard would need the charger, but he didn't carry it in the truck. He'd charged the battery recently, so it should be good for a few more days. The next time he came, he'd bring the charger.

He glanced toward the roof of Richard's house and wondered if electricity had been wired to all rooms or just the kitchen. Best he check it right now and see if he needed to bring out an extension cord.

When he got inside, he presented Richard with the cell phone. The boy studied the instrument intently. Hawkman showed him how to dial, then placed it on the boy's ear. He pointed out the feel of the vibrations and Richard nodded vigorously. Hawkman flipped the phone to vibrator and attached it to Richard's belt. Jennifer wrote down the instructions along with Hawkman's home, office and beeper numbers.

They searched for working electrical outlets throughout the house. Richard found one in his room. Hawkman found two outlets in the living room, then headed for Francine's room, but gave it a second thought and turned away. No need to invade that space at this time.

When Hawkman and Jennifer prepared to leave, Richard thanked them profusely and shoved fifteen dollars into Hawkman's hand. He started to refuse the money, but noticed the pleading look in Richard's eyes and stuck it in his pocket.

On the way home, he handed the bills to Jennifer. "Save this for Richard. He'll need it later."

Richard watched them leave and waved from the front porch, grateful for having met such nice people. He watched until the truck disappeared, then headed straight for the kitchen where he opened one of the loaves of fresh bread and inhaled the aroma. Then he reached for the jar of peanut butter and dug into the creamy paste with a big spoon. He spread it thick on one piece of bread, then smeared honey on another slice, making a sticky, gooey sandwich. Pouring a tall glass of milk, he sat down at the table, took a big bite and closed his eyes. He felt he'd gone to heaven, as he hadn't tasted anything so good in over a week.

Glancing down at the empty floor, a surge of sadness slid through his chest. He could visualize Ruffy sitting beside him, begging with those big black eyes. Richard took a deep breath and pushed the gloomy thoughts from his mind. Those images would only drive him crazy.

He ate quickly, then went outside to tend the animals. Unrolling the hose, he watered the vegetables, so glad his dad had plumbed a line from the well for mom's garden. Three years ago they'd had to carry buckets from the stream or the well, just to keep the plants alive. It still made his back ache when he thought of that chore. He walked the rows of plants giving the soil one more drenching before turning off the water. Suddenly, he had that strange sensation of being watched and turned quickly, only to see Whitey standing by the gate, looking mighty lonesome.

Richard remembered the bowl of fruit Jennifer had placed on the table and dashed into the house. Grabbing an apple, he hurried back to the barn yard and sat on the gate leading to the small pasture. He peeled the fruit with his knife, watching Whitey out of the corner of his eye.

The horse shook his mane and nudged his arm. Grinning, Richard let the apple peel hang loose, but held the fruit close to his chest. It only took a few seconds before Whitey shoved his wet nose under the boy's arm and nibbled at the treat. Richard laughed and grabbed the horse's mane, pulling himself onto the steed's back. He took a few bites of the apple, then held out the remaining tidbit to the horse. Whitey munched as he carried his passenger at a slow walk into the field.

Giving the mount a gentle pat on the neck, Richard recalled the day his dad brought this beloved animal home and how happy it had made his mom. She'd ridden in horse shows as a girl and taught

Richard to ride. He and she would double up and ride bareback for hours around the area. The horse had been trained well. With a soft heel to the flank, they could run him through several smooth and easy paces. If you touched his chest, he'd kneel on his front legs so one could mount or dismount with ease.

Richard lay forward against Whitey's neck. Stroking him gently, he found peace in the closeness of the horse's warm body. Dear friend, he thought, I'm glad you're here and gave the horse a hug.

❉•❉•❉•❉•❉

The next day, Hawkman decided to go to his office in Medford. Frank Alberts made him uneasy and he wanted to know why the interest in Richard. When he'd asked Williams about the situation, the detective shook his head, claiming the officer to be a crude character with a clean record, just doing a little more than his job required. He explained that Alberts had left the force in southern California because he couldn't stand the pressure.

But Hawkman's better sense suggested more than nerves. He called Kevin Louis, a retired policeman who helped out at the station and also aided Hawkman on many of his cases. He requested a background search on Alberts since he had access to the police computers.

After hanging up from Kevin, the phone immediately rang.

"Mr. Casey, Detective Williams here."

"Hey, Williams, call me Hawkman. My clients call me Mr. Casey."

Williams laughed. "Okay, Hawkman. Just wondered if you knew of any relatives of the Cliffords in this area?"

"No. I didn't know the family before this tragedy. But I'll speak with Richard. In fact, I'll drop by the Zanker's ranch first. He seems close to the boy and might have some information."

"Thanks, Hawkman. We need to get in touch with someone. The boy's under age and I'm not sure how long we can leave him out there without adult supervision."

"You can't take Richard from that farm," Hawkman said. "It's all he's got. It would devastate him."

"Then we've got to get a court assigned guardian if we can't find a relative. That's the law."

"I'll get back to you as soon as I find out anything."

"Uh, Hawkman. You realize, I'm not hiring you. The Department can't afford it."

He laughed. "Don't worry detective. I've got this compassion streak I can't seem to control and sometimes do police work for free."

The detective chuckled. "Thanks. I'll remember that."

Hawkman decided not to wait for the Alberts report and left word for Kevin to fax it to his house. He figured it more important to get out to Zankers' before dark and see what he could uncover. He slapped on his leather cowboy hat, shrugged on his jeans jacket and left.

From Medford, it took him close to three hours to get out to the Zanker ranch. The two dogs rushed out barking and gnashing their teeth in a threatening manner. Hawkman stepped out of the 4X4 and commanded them to sit. The dogs obeyed and wagged their tails when he threw each of them a doggy treat.

Herb stepped out the front door and laughed loudly. "My word, you know how to tame the most vicious."

Hawkman smiled. "I've seen you with those two wimps. They're all bark and no bite."

Herb motioned for him to have a seat. "Got time for a beer."

"Sounds good."

The two men sat on the front porch and Elsie brought them out two cold beers with frosty mugs.

"Hello, Hawkman," she said. "How's Jennifer?"

"She's busy meeting her deadlines."

"I love reading her nature articles. She's such a good writer. Is her mystery series coming out soon?"

Hawkman nodded. "Probably in six months to a year. She's working hard to get them completed."

"You tell her I'll be looking forward to those books."

"I'll do that, Mrs. Zanker."

"Please excuse me, I've ironing to finish."

Elsie went back into the house and Herb turned to Hawkman. "Now, what brings you out here this afternoon?"

Hawkman took a gulp of beer and wiped his mouth with the back of his hand. "Do you know if Richard has any kin folks in the area?"

Herb shook his head. "Bob's brother, Joe, used to live in Montague. But after Bob passed away, he left the area. Francine didn't say much about him, other than he'd moved back to the Midwest somewhere. Maybe Richard knows."

"What about her folks?"

"From what I understand, she was an only child and both her parents passed away several years ago. All she had were Bob and Richard." Herb shook his head and frowned. "Sad, isn't it?"

"Yeah," Hawkman said. "And the law states that Richard can't live out there alone. He's under age."

Herb jerked his head up. "Oh my God, I hadn't thought about that. But you're right. A guardian will have to be picked. Well, that's no problem. Elsie and I will do it. Then the boy can stay on his own place as my ranch hand. I'll pay him a small salary to make everything legal."

"That's fine, but is that his property? Do they owe money on it? Everything will have to go through probate. And if the place isn't paid for, it could be taken away from him and sold to pay any outstanding debts."

Herb stood up. "Bob Clifford had the insight to take out a mortgage that paid the place off in the event of his death. So Francine owned the place free and clear. But we should go over there, find the papers and make sure everything gets put into Richard's name. I hope this doesn't get sticky. I don't want that boy to lose the only thing he has left."

"Especially when the system finds out he's deaf."

# CHAPTER SIX

*Herb clasped his hands behind his back as they walked toward* Hawkman's truck. "You know, when I grew up, men were married and raising families at Richard's age."

"Times have changed, Herb. Without a guardian, this boy won't have a chance to stay on that place until he's eighteen. So, we'll have to go to bat for him."

Herb slammed the truck door. "Elsie and I are ready to do just that."

Driving over to the Clifford place, Hawkman chewed on a toothpick. "By the way, Herb, do you happen to know where Richard's mother will be buried?"

"Yes. I've talked with the coroner. They won't be releasing her body for a spell. But when they do, I've made arrangements that she be buried next to her husband, Bob."

Hawkman glanced at the man's sad face. "That's very kind of you, Herb. Have you told the boy?"

"Not yet. I just made the funeral plans today. I've also arranged for the dog to be cremated and Richard can have the ashes to scatter where he wishes. The boy has lost everything he loved. It breaks my heart."

Hawkman nodded. "I know the boy will be relieved. I'm sure it's been on his mind."

"I intend to talk to him today."

When they pulled up to the house, Hawkman started to honk, then realized that would be futile. Richard would sense their presence. But when they got out of the truck, they didn't see him anywhere.

Hawkman cocked his head and swore he could hear the churning of motorcycles, but Richard's bike sat parked in the barn. Then suddenly he heard the frightened neigh of a horse. Whirling around, he yanked open the truck door and jumped back inside. "Herb, get in, there's something going on in the field."

Herb quickly climbed back into the 4X4 and Hawkman floored the accelerator. He sped up the small hill and when he crested the top, he saw the problem. Two cyclists were circling a scared Richard mounted bare back on his horse, Whitey.

Hawkman reached inside his jacket and flipped up the flap on his shoulder holster. The noise of the motorcycles prevented their riders from hearing the truck until it pulled between them and the horse. The dust settled and it became deathly quiet. Richard leaped off Whitey and ran to the 4X4. "Boy, am I glad to see you."

Hawkman stepped onto the ground, patted the boy on the shoulder and strolled toward one of the bikers. Richard leaned against the fender and watched. The scroungy looking man flung his leg over the seat of his cycle and stood beside it while wrapping a chain around his hand. He raised his arm as if to strike until he saw the gun aimed at his belly. Dropping his hand, he backed off.

"Hey man, we didn't do no harm."

Hawkman glared at him. "You're on private property. I want you out of here by the time I count to three."

The two men hustled to get on their bikes.

"One-two-three." Hawkman fired and flattened the back tires of both bikes. "Aah, too bad. You weren't fast enough. Now you'll just have to push those babies all the way back to where you came from."

One of the men made a threatening move. But, Hawkman fired at the ground in front of him, causing dirt to pelt the man's bare shins. Dancing around, he grabbed the handle bars and started pushing the bike toward the road. Hawkman memorized the license plates as the men grunted and groaned up the hill. Before they were out of sight, sweat glistened off their arms and had soaked through the backs of their leather vest.

Hawkman waved his hand to get Richard's attention. "Where'd they come from?"

Richard shrugged. "I don't know."

"Have you ever seen them before?"

He pointed toward the hills. "Three weeks ago. I saw those two with a couple of women up there. I told mom about them and she wouldn't let me go riding for three days. She said they were scum."

"Did she know them?"

Richard shook his head. "She just figured they were up to no good."

"Smart woman. Glad you listened to her." Hawkman glanced down at Richard's belt. "Where's the cell phone?"

"In my room."

"You should have it on. I want you to wear it at all times. I've brought the charger and an extra battery." Hawkman gestured toward the truck. "Want to ride back with us?"

Richard waved him off. "No, I'll ride Whitey. He's still jumpy. I need to calm him down."

Hawkman admired the boy's compassion for the animal and watched him touch the horse's chest. Whitey kneeled on his front legs, allowing Richard to hop easily onto his back. The boy smiled as the horse came back upon his feet. With a small stick he touched the horse's flank and they started toward the house in a smooth cantor.

Herb stuck his head out the window and smiled. "Now, isn't that a sight?"

Hawkman, his expression solemn, climbed into the truck and turned on the ignition. "I don't like those bikers hanging around here. They're the type that are usually hiding from the law and are nothing but trouble."

Frowning, Herb nodded. "That's true. They seem to seek out these isolated areas, creating havoc until they're caught and thrown back into jail."

"None too soon for my liking," Hawkman said, as he topped the hill. He could still see the men in the distance pushing their bikes down the dirt road.

They reached the house about the same time Richard galloped into the barn yard. As he jumped off the horse, he called out, "I'll meet you in the house. Need to wipe him down."

Hawkman and Herb went inside and sat down at the kitchen table. Richard joined them shortly.

"Thanks, Hawkman. You saved my life."

"I don't think they were out to kill you. Maybe scare you a bit. They were just getting their kicks."

"They should feel plenty of kicks, cause I was mighty scared."

Hawkman moved his head to conceal a grin. When he glanced back at Richard, he caught him staring at his shoulder holster.

"Are you a spy?"

Hawkman pulled out his .38, and the boy stepped back, his eyes wide. "Years ago I used to be with the Agency. But not after I got injured." He pointed to the eye-patch. "Now I'm a private investigator."

"How did that happen?"

"Long story, I'll tell you another time. Right now Mr. Zanker needs to talk to you."

Herb took hold of Richard's arm and led him to the couch in the living room. Sitting down next to him, he explained where the boy's mother would be buried as soon as the police released her body and about the dog's ashes.

Richard nodded sadly. "Thank you, Mr. Zanker. I feel better knowing mom will be with dad."

Herb took a deep breath. "Now, son, we need to find your Uncle Joe."

Richard shrugged. "I don't know where he is."

Hawkman had come in quietly and stepped in front of the boy. "Didn't you get letters from him?"

Again, he shrugged. "If mom heard from him, she didn't tell me."

"May we look in her things?" Hawkman asked.

Richard's face pinched in agony and his gaze shifted toward the door to his mother's room. "I guess. But I don't want to go in there."

"You don't have to. We'll be very careful not to disturb anything. We're just going to look for any mail or an address book, plus we need to find the papers on this house so we can get everything changed into your name."

Richard furrowed his brow. "Then why do you need to find Uncle Joe?"

Hawkman knew the truth would be shocking, but he wasn't about to lie. "We need to find your next of kin or the law could force you off this land until you're eighteen."

A look of horror passed across the boy's face. "No. This is my place now. I have to stay here. Everything will die without me."

Hawkman raised his hand in a sign of comfort. "I know. And we'll do everything we can. It would just make things easier if we could find your uncle. Or some other adult kinfolk. Is there anyone else we could get in touch with?"

Richard frowned. "No. He's all that's left."

Hawkman hesitated a moment before he and Herb moved into Francine's room. They carefully went through every drawer for some clue of Uncle Joe's whereabouts. In their rummaging they came across close to one hundred dollars that Francine had stashed in various areas. They piled the money on the dresser to give to Richard after they'd exhausted their search. Hawkman had just about given up when he spotted a small shoe box on the top closet shelf and pulled it down. Inside, along with a couple of envelopes, he found a small address book. The letters were addressed to Francine. The return only had "Joe".

"Herb, I might have hit pay dirt here." He sat down on the only chair in the room and looked at the letters first. One had an Oklahoma postmark, the more recent one, Kansas. Opening the latter, he read the short note and raised his brows. "No wonder Francine didn't tell Richard about his uncle. He's in jail."

"What?" Herb exclaimed, moving swiftly to Hawkman's side.

"A DUI. Jailed for thirty days. But he's bound to be out now, as this appears to have been written over a month ago. Says he's going to Wichita in hopes of getting a job. I'll get on the computer tonight and see if I can locate him."

Herb rubbed his chin. "It's amazing what you can do on the Internet."

"Yep, technology has come a long way." Hawkman flipped through the little address book and found it full of money figures instead of addresses. He studied it for a moment, then showed it to Herb. "This looks like a record of mortgage payments paid before Bob's death, but I don't see the deed." He glanced back to the closet. "There's another shoe box up there. Let's see what it holds."

Herb stepped over to the closet and pulled it down. He took off the lid and glanced through the papers. "Looks like the deed is here, plus some correspondence to the Veterans. Which reminds me, I better get in touch with them soon, so there won't be a break in Richard's checks."

Hawkman examined the contents. "At least the house is paid off. That will be one burden Richard won't have to worry about. Once the check comes in his name, he'll be able to pretty well fend for himself until he can get a job." He closed the lid and tucked the box under his arm.

"That's good," Herb nodded. "I'll tell Richard what we found and our plans. He'll be relieved for us to take over these matters."

Hawkman took the money off the dresser and the two men left the room, closing the door behind them. They explained the situation to the boy, and gave him the bills they'd found. Richard happily consented to let them work out his financial and property affairs.

When Hawkman arrived home, he went straight to his computer at the back of the house and started searching the Wichita, Kansas area for Joseph Clifford. He found many and thumped his fist on the table. "Damn, I forgot to ask Richard his uncle's full name and I can't call him to find out."

He printed out the addresses and phone numbers of those that looked like they could be Joe Clifford, then attempted some calls. After two hours of a futile search, he took out his atlas and checked the surrounding area. His instinct zeroed in on a small town called Derby. Not sure why that name attracted him, he went to the computer and keyed it in on the search engine. A Joseph Kenneth Clifford popped up. It sounded right. He punched in the given phone number and a sleepy voice came over the line.

"Hello. Is this Joe Clifford, the brother of the now deceased Bob Clifford from the Copco Lake area?"

"I don't know. Who's this?"

"My name's Tom Casey. I'm a private investigator, looking for the next of kin of Richard Clifford."

"Yeah, that's my nephew. What's the problem?"

"Unfortunately, I have bad news."

"The kid okay?"

"Yes, the boy's fine. But his mother, Francine has been murdered."

"What!"

Hawkman felt the man immediately come awake.

"Oh, my God! What happened?"

"Richard found her and the dog on the kitchen floor with their throats slashed when he returned from a motorcycle ride in the hills."

"Dear Lord! What kind of an animal would do that? Have you found the murderer?"

"No. But, unfortunately, Richard is suspect."

"That's impossible! That boy wouldn't have harmed his mother or that dog."

"I believe you. The boy tried to contact a neighbor for several days, but they were gone on vacation. He finally had to get the bodies out of the house, so he buried the dog and put his mother in the grain bin in the barn."

"Oh, no! That poor kid."

"Mr. Clifford, the reason I called is that Richard is still a minor and can't stay at the house without an adult present."

"Hell, he's old enough to take care of that dinky place."

"I agree with you, but the law sees it differently."

"Are you suggesting I come back there?"

"Only until the boy turns eighteen. If you don't, the property could be taken away from him."

"You're talking about staying there for a year."

"That's true, but if you can't do that, maybe you could at least come back long enough to appoint a guardian. I know of several people who would be interested in helping out in that manner."

"Could I do it by mail?"

"Mr. Clifford, don't you think you owe it to the boy to be back here with him while he's struggling through this tragedy?"

"That's not the point, Mr. Casey. If I come back there, I could be killed too."

# CHAPTER SEVEN

*There were several moments of silence before either man spoke.*
Finally, Hawkman cleared his throat. "Mr. Clifford, I guess I don't understand. Are you saying the same person that murdered Mrs. Clifford might kill you too?"

Joe exhaled a long breath. "I'm not saying the same person. But I owe a good sum of money to someone who used to live in that area. When I started receiving threatening phone calls and Bob's family got menacing mail, I decided to get the hell out of there. I certainly couldn't earn any money to repay the debt if I was dead or in jail."

"If he doesn't reside here anymore, it shouldn't be a problem. We certainly won't advertise your presence."

"Wish I could count on that, but it doesn't seem to matter because wherever I went in California or Oregon, he found me. That's why I skipped out and went clear across country and never let anyone know where I ended up. I know it sounds cruel, but that's the way it had to be."

"Could you give me the name of this person, so I can check on him. Maybe he did kill Francine."

"I doubt he'd go as far as murder, but I guess anything's possible. His name is Hal Jenkins. The last I heard he lived in southern California and worked as a police officer in that area. How he ever got that job, I'll never know. A real clod of a guy."

Hawkman stiffened and wrote down the name on a piece of

paper and circled the word "clod" several times. "If there's some way you can make it out here to visit Richard, if only for a few days, please let me know. Here's my phone number. Otherwise, I'll look into what can be done legally through the mail on appointing a guardian for the boy."

"Thanks Mr. Casey. I'll keep in touch. I feel horrible about what's happened. Tell Richard hello for me and that I love him. But until I can get my problems solved, I won't be seeing him. Please don't tell him where I am."

The phone clicked and Hawkman stared at the dead instrument. What kind of a man could leave a young boy to fend for himself after the murder of his only living parent? He had the feeling that Richard knew his uncle pretty well.

⫷-╫-╫-╫-╫-⫸

After hanging up the phone, Joe Clifford sat with his head in his hands for a long time. Tears spilled from his eyes, made their way between his fingers and dropped onto the carpet. What kind of a human being am I anyway, he thought. That boy's all that's left of my only brother's family. And deaf at that. I'm so scared about what could be waiting for me, that I can't go back to be with that poor kid. He's out there taking care of himself, being more of a man than I am. Bob raised him right.

Joe wiped his nose with the back of his sleeve and suddenly an idea occurred to him. I'll send Bob's guns to Richard. That will make up for my not going back. He knows more about firearms than I do and can protect himself.

His heart lifted and he immediately pulled the hard cases that contained the guns from his closet. He smiled when he opened one and examined the Beretta A 390 ST 12 ga. What a beautiful shotgun. At least he'd kept it clean and rust free since Bob had put him in charge.

Then he clicked open the smaller case with the Beretta Series 92 pistol that had the 11 round magazine, plus a cable lock. "That's a darlin'," he said aloud, picking up the gun.

Last, he checked the 30.06 Ruger rifle. Satisfied they were all clean and ready to be shipped, Joe closed the cases. Richard would get many years of use from these beautiful guns. Joe thought back on how Bob had obtained them. His brother could never have purchased these expensive guns outright, but he'd done a lot of work for a man who'd lost money in a law suit. In exchange for Bob's labor, the man gave him the guns. Bob felt he'd gotten more than if he'd been paid.

Joe thought about how proud the boy would be to get these back. The poor kid probably figured he'd never see them again. What a surprise he'll get when the package arrives. He grinned, picturing Richard opening the box. A great kid. Even though deaf, he was smart as a whip and used his other senses to the fullest so that he could probably feel, smell and see better than most animals.

It took Joe a couple of days to find the right size box and packing material. Finally, the day came when he mailed it. He stood outside the Federal Express thinking about the boy's expression when he opened the prize. It made him feel better to know that Richard would now have some protection.

He'd keep in touch with Mr. Casey and hopefully be able to help Richard without having to go back, risking his own life. Feeling better and with a much lighter heart, Joe Clifford headed for work.

⸙⸙⸙⸙⸙⸙

Hawkman received a phone message from Uncle Joe. Not only did he fear for his life, but he'd lose his job, so he wouldn't be coming to Oregon. But please keep him updated. He also told Hawkman that a large package would be arriving for Richard soon.

The man's decision didn't surprise Hawkman. He'd heard the fear in his voice on the phone. But what the hell would he be sending Richard? He hoped it would somehow make up for the loss of Uncle Joe's support. But he doubted it.

Kevin had faxed the report about Frank Alberts before he and his wife left for a week's trip back to North Dakota to see their new grandson. Hawkman needed Kevin's expertise in searching out this Hal Jenkins that Joe owed money to, so he'd have to wait. But meanwhile, he'd see if he could help Herb expedite the legal paperwork for the appointment of a guardian. They'd just have to send it to Joe Clifford for his signature.

Hawkman returned home that evening, newspaper tucked under his arm and found a note from Jennifer explaining she'd gone to an auxiliary meeting of the volunteer fire fighters wives. So, when the phone rang, he figured it would be for her and let the machine pick up. But when Richard's frightened voice came over the line, it definitely caught his attention.

"Hawkman, motorcycles back."

The newspaper fell to the floor as Hawkman raced out the door and jumped into the truck. Racing across the bridge, he spun left up Ager Beswick and drove as fast as he dared over the narrow and rough road. It would take him at least fifteen minutes to get to Richard's house. Sweat beaded his forehead. Why were those two motorcycle guys so intent on harassing a kid? Unless they thought he knew something.

Not knowing how many he might encounter, he decided to call the sheriff. He spoke Sheriff Daniel's number into the new hands free cell phone that he'd purchased after giving Richard his old one. The sheriff assured him a back-up would be sent to Clifford's immediately.

Hawkman thought the old log road would never come into view and skidded around the sharp turn. It was still light out and clouds of dirt encircled the house. His heart pounding, Hawkman pulled his gun from underneath his jacket and threw off the safety. As he pulled up to the front approach, he could hear the familiar pinging of a twenty-two coming from the back of the house.

Richard must have barricaded himself inside. Not wanting to take a chance of frightening the boy or getting shot while trying to get to him, Hawkman drove across the yard and headed for the back. Two motorcyclists were riding back and forth across the garden, rooting up the tender plants that Richard had worked so hard to keep alive.

Hawkman felt the heat surge through his body as he burned with rage. Aiming his gun at the bikes, he fired four times, blowing out both tires of each cycle. One man flew over the handle bars, coming down hard on his shoulder, screaming in pain as he rolled around on the hard ground. The other bike twisted about, throwing the man off and the heavy machine came to rest on the lower half of his body. Hawkman jumped out of the truck, his gun poised.

"You two are definitely slow learners."

Both men groaned when they glanced up. "It's the damn one-eyed Jack again," one said, as he struggled to his knees, holding his shoulder.

"Just stay where you are," Hawkman instructed.

The man plopped back on his rear in the dirt.

Richard appeared at the back door, his gun resting across his arm. At that moment, Hawkman heard a siren in the distance and glanced toward the road, Richard's eyes followed his gaze. The car squealed at the turn and came to a dusty stop.

Frank Alberts jumped out of the patrol car, his gun drawn, his partner at his heels. "Looks like we've got a couple of problems on motorcycles." He turned his gun on the man holding his shoulder. "What the hell are you doing here, messin' with a kid? Don't you have the guts to pick on a man?" Alberts kicked his heel along the ground, sending dirt into the man's eyes. "I'd advise you to get on your feet."

Groaning, the cyclist, rolled over on his good side and pushed himself into a standing position. "We didn't harm no one."

"Like hell you didn't. You scared the boy to death." The officer turned and looked at the other man. "And look at that garden. What's the matter with you two? If you had any sense at all, you'd know that boy could have grown enough food in about a month to fill your stupid ass stomachs. You ain't got no sense at all. Get your lazy asses up. Rogers, cuff 'em."

Alberts strolled over toward Richard and looked up at him standing on the steps. "You okay, boy?"

Richard nodded.

Then the officer went to Hawkman. "Mr. Casey. I've learned a few things about you since I saw you last. Sorry I've been so stupid. Hope you accept my apology. I'll get these scum out of here and I'll send a tow truck in to get these cycles. If they want 'em when they get out of jail for disturbin' the peace and trespassin', they'll have to pay a hearty sum."

Hawkman scratched his head and watched the officer push the two into the back seat of his patrol car and take off. He glanced up at Richard and shrugged.

Richard rested his gun against the door and walked solemnly down the steps toward the garden. He bent down and tenderly tried to right the broken plants.

Hawkman felt his heart squeeze. "Tomorrow, we'll get some plants to replace them."

But the boy wasn't looking at him.

Hawkman walked over and put a hand on his shoulder. Richard looked up, the corners of his mouth turned down. "I don't think I can save them."

# CHAPTER EIGHT

*Later that night, tears welled in Jennifer's eyes as Hawkman told* her how the boy's garden had been destroyed.

She exhaled a puff of air that ruffled her bangs. "I don't understand grown men getting their kicks that way. "Why were they so determined to scare Richard?

Hawkman shook his head. "I'm not sure. Unless, they had something to do with Francine's murder."

Jennifer whirled around, her eyes wide. "Do you think that's possible?

"It's sure strange they picked a lone kid to terrorize. I keep asking myself, why? Unless, they fear Richard saw something."

She grabbed his arm. "Hawkman, that boy can't stay out there alone. It's too dangerous. There are more guys like those two up in the hills. They're like a pack of wild animals."

"True, but it's been the same two that have harassed Richard several times. That's what makes me suspicious. Fortunately, they're going to be in jail awhile. Believe it or not, Alberts answered the call and took those two away. And he appeared pretty ticked."

She waved a hand in the air and rolled her eyes. "You mean that horrid policeman?"

"Yeah. He even apologized to me and acted compassionately toward Richard."

"Well, that's a definite change. Wonder what brought that on?"

"I don't know." Hawkman scratched his side burn. "Bowled me over. I don't quite know what to think about his shift in attitude. Anyway, I think Richard will be okay for now. I'm going to take him into town tomorrow and refurbish his garden."

Jennifer smiled and gave him a hug. "Good. You want me to go?"

"Not really. This will give me an opportunity to get to know Richard better. More on a man to man basis."

"You're right." Then her gaze fell to the counter and she reached for an envelope. "Oh! I almost forgot. We got a letter from Sam." Handing it to him, she continued. "His boss is kind enough to let him have some time off, so he's going to get to come home for a few days before the university starts its fall session. He's almost through with summer school and doing well. So, sometime in August we'll get to see him. He's not sure of the date yet." She shook her head. "Kids, you'd think they'd be more. . ." Then she stopped and tapped her finger against her chin.

Hawkman glanced up from reading. "They'd be more what?"

"I just remembered something Sam told me last year."

"Go on."

She leaned her elbows on the kitchen bar opposite him. "I bet Sam knows Richard."

He raised a brow. "How?"

"Remember when he used to go up in the hills on his dirt bike, staying for hours and we'd worry about him?"

He nodded. "Yeah."

"Well, he told me once that there was this kid he'd see up there once in awhile riding a dirt bike. So they'd race through the hills together. He said they seldom talked, just rode. He never found out the boy's name or knew where he lived. But, when the boy spoke, his voice sounded strange."

Hawkman listened with interest. "That certainly sounds like Richard all right. I'll ask Sam when he gets home."

❖❀❖❀❖❀❖❀❖

The next morning, Richard hurried through his chores, knowing Hawkman would be there about mid-morning. He'd reworked the garden soil and had it ready for the new plants. After showering, he fixed a big breakfast of fresh eggs and fried the remaining bacon from the package Jennifer had brought. It wouldn't be long before he'd be able to take care of himself and not have to depend on people to bring him food. He and Mr. Zanker had filled out all the necessary forms for the Veteran's check and it should start coming in his name very soon. Of course, he first had to pay back Mr. Zanker for taking care of some outstanding bills that had come in the mail. But he had the amount stored in his head.

In his haste at cleaning up his mess, he dropped the cap off the chocolate syrup and it went rolling under the refrigerator. Kneeling, he ran his hand under the appliance and came out with not only the cap, but a strange looking metal button that looked dirty. Richard started to rinse it off, but something stopped him. That didn't look like ordinary dirt on that button. It appeared more like dried blood. The thought made his insides seize up and his hand trembled. Grabbing a small plastic sack lying on the drainboard, he quickly dropped the button inside. He held the bag toward the window and stared for several seconds, wondering where that button had come from. Sealing it with a tie, he dropped to his knees in front of the lower cabinet, reached inside toward the far corner and fished out the paper sack containing the liquor bottle he'd found under the bushes. One of these days, he'd show these items to someone he could trust. He hoped he'd find that person soon, as he knew the longer a murder stayed unsolved, the harder it became to find the guilty party.

Richard shoved the sack back into the cabinet and wiped down the table. Then feeling the vibrations of a heavy vehicle pulling up out front, he glanced out the window. When he saw Hawkman jump out of the truck, he tossed the dishrag into the sink, excitement welling in his chest as he hurried to the door.

❖❖❖❖❖

The two climbed into the vehicle, ready for the trip to town. Hawkman had left on the radio. But before he had a chance to punch it off, Richard pressed both hands over the speakers. Hawkman watched with interest as the boy twisted the knob to a station playing the latest music. Immediately, he bobbed his head up and down, keeping perfect time with the beat. Hawkman smiled, wondering how else this boy would amaze him.

"You like music?"

Richard nodded and grinned, then quickly turned off the radio. "Sorry, it's probably too loud."

"No, it's fine if you want to listen." Regretting his words, Hawkman started the engine and headed down the road. An old beat up Ford pick-up coming the opposite direction passed them. Hawkman noticed Richard eyeing the truck.

"Who's that?" Hawkman asked.

"Jerome."

"I've never seen him around. Where does he live."

Richard turned and pointed out the back window. "About a half mile or so on up the logging road past my house. He hasn't been home for several days. I tried to find him when mom. . ." He hesitated for a moment, then continued. "When I needed help."

"What's his last name?"

Richard shrugged. "I don't know. We just always called him 'hermit of the hill'.

"He lives alone?"

"I guess. I've never seen anyone with him but his mangy old black dog, Midnight."

"Is the man friendly?"

Richard told him about Jerome coming to see his ill father, bringing fruit from his trees and vegetables from the produce markets in town. The man had continued the visits for awhile after his dad died, but he hadn't seen him in several months. He omitted telling that he thought Jerome had a crush on his mother. At the moment it seemed petty and juvenile. He didn't want to appear immature.

Hawkman changed the subject and got Richard talking about the garden and what types of plants he had growing when the bikers destroyed them. He instructed the boy to write down what they would need to get the garden back to its original shape.

When they reached Yreka, they went to several different nurseries to find everything. And it took a lot of talking from Hawkman to convince Richard to let him pay the bill. He finally convinced him by agreeing that he and Jennifer would accept some of the first yield as payment. Only then did Richard put his money back into his pocket.

After going to the drive-thru at the fast food place, they headed back to plant the garden. Hawkman grinned watching out of the corner of his eye as the boy devoured the hamburger and fries. They reached the Clifford house late in the afternoon and the two worked on the garden for a couple of hours. After bedding the last plants and making sure each had a good dose of plant Vitamin B to prevent shock, Hawkman waved goodbye.

Richard stood back and admired the newly restored garden. He felt the plants were healthier looking than the ones he had before and would bear better. Pleased with the accomplishment, he gathered his tools and rested them against the house in case he needed them tomorrow. He noticed Old Betsy standing at the gate waiting to be milked, so he ran into the house and got his bucket. Tonight, he'd use the separator and get some rich cream.

He let Betsy into the barn yard, patting her nose as she munched the grain in his other hand. She followed him inside and put her head into the trough where he'd placed some pieces of hay and a bit more grain. He closed the opening so she couldn't pull her head out and knock over the bucket before he finished. Sitting down on his three legged stool, he started milking. A stray cat had found its way into his barn and periodically he would squirt a stream of milk into it's mouth, laughing aloud at its antics as it rolled over on its back and purred. A cat would keep the varmints out of the grain, so he welcomed the little critter.

He'd just about finished, when something made him jerk his head around. Gasping, he jumped up and almost knocked over the bucket of milk. What looked like the silhouette of a giant stood in the center of the barn's large door. Richard couldn't see the man's face, but recognized his visitor at a glance.

# CHAPTER NINE

*The big man stepped into the barn, his coat flapping in the* breeze. He placed his hands on his hips and stopped. Richard could see those strange blue eyes glowing in the shadows.

"Hello, Jerome."

"Where's your mother? I need to talk to her."

Richard's gaze dropped to the full bucket of milk in front of Betsy's hooves. He moved it out of the way, then released the cow's neck from the manger, giving her a gentle push toward the door.

Jerome stepped so close that Richard could smell his sweat and sour breath.

"Mom's gone." He picked up the bucket, brushing his shoulder against the man as he headed for the house. Jerome twisted around and hurried along at Richard's heels, puffing like a steam engine.

Once they were in the kitchen and Richard had placed the milk on the kitchen table, Jerome gripped the boy's shoulder, turned him around and stared into Richard's face. "What do you mean your mother's gone?" he spat.

"Someone killed her and Ruffy."

Jerome dropped his hand and stumbled backwards, practically falling into a kitchen chair. "Someone murdered them?"

Richard pointed at the floor. "I found her and Ruffy here." A lump formed in his throat just thinking about that horrible day. He turned away, blinking back the tears as he set to work putting the separator together. Once he'd regained his composure, he faced Jerome. "I came up to your place several times, but never found you home."

"I've been gone," Jerome said, rubbing a dirty sleeve across his mouth and beard. "Why would anyone want to kill your mother? She didn't have any money."

Richard shot a look at him, thinking, it might have been more than money they wanted, you old fool. Suddenly, his eyes focused on the missing brass buttons on Jerome's tattered coat. He caught his breath and quickly turned back to putting the separator together.

Finally, Jerome heaved himself out of the chair and shuffled toward the front door. Richard watched him leave from the window, his eyes narrowing as his gaze followed the old pick-up until it turned up the road and disappeared. He dropped down to his knees in front of the cabinet and fished out the sack from the far corner. Careful not to touch the liquor bottle, he lifted the small plastic bag from inside and studied the brass looking button. Holding it up toward the light, he couldn't tell for sure if it matched the ones on Jerome's coat. Too much dirt or blood covered the design. He let out a sigh and dropped it back inside. It made him wonder if Jerome had left the day before or after his mother had been murdered?

He finished separating the milk and found himself with a good amount of rich cream. Betsy had done well. He stored it in the refrigerator then went outside and closed up the chicken coop. A full moon lit up the yard, so he sat on the porch for a while and sharpened his knife on the whet stone. He stared off in the distance toward Jerome's place.

⊹❖⊹❖⊹❖⊹❖⊹

When Hawkman arrived home, Jennifer knew he had something on his mind. "How'd everything go?"

"Great. Richard's garden is probably better than before."

"Then what's troubling you."

He glanced at her and grinned. "Can't keep a thing from you, can I?"

She laughed. "Nope."

He sat down on one of the stools on the opposite side of the kitchen bar and watched as she prepared dinner. "There's a man called Jerome that lives up past Richard's house. A hermit, from what the boy said. Richard went to his place for help several times, but never found the man home."

"So why does that bother you?"

"I don't know. But I think I'm going to pay the hermit a visit and ask him a few questions. From what Richard told me, Jerome visited the family on several occasions before Mr. Clifford died. However, I got the feeling, that he made some visits after Clifford's death. Richard said he hadn't seen him for some time. So why would the man quit coming?" he asked thoughtfully.

"You're always so full of questions."

He shrugged. "It's my job. Just like yours when you have to get information for your articles."

She smiled. "You're right. And you're wondering why the visits stopped?"

Hawkman nodded. "Yeah, it bothers me. Think I'll go into town and talk to Williams about Jerome. See if he can give me some information on this guy. Then I'm going over to the jail and question those two bikers."

"Sounds like a good start," Jennifer said, placing a full plate of food in front of him.

His face lit up like fireworks when he eyed the large steak, baked potato and salad. "Oh, man, does that look delicious."

The next morning, Hawkman drove into Yreka and stopped at the police station. He poked his head around the door jam of the detective's office and found him bent over his desk, busily filling out forms.

"Hey, Williams, why aren't you out working?"

The detective scowled. "If it weren't for all this damned paperwork, we might get something done. Just finished filling out all the data on those two bikers. Got their cycles towed in and when they get out of jail, they'll have to lay out a pretty penny to get those babies back. They won't be bothering anybody for some time." He waved Hawkman in. "Have a seat."

"That's one thing I wanted to talk to you about. What'd those guys have to say when you questioned them? Give you any clue as to why they were harassing Richard?"

Williams slumped back in his chair and ran his fingers through his hair. "I guess Francine Clifford was quite a looker. Seems like our motorcycle chumps saw her out in the field one day and tried to flirt with her. She turned them off like a cold bucket of water and they didn't like that. So they decided to teach her a lesson. I doubt they had the slightest inkling the women was deaf.

However, I don't think they realized the woman had been murdered, because when we read them their rights and told them they were suspects in her murder, they came unglued at the news." He slapped his fist on the desk. "But that type can put on such a good act."

Hawkman agreed. "You can't believe them, that's for sure. By the way, are you familiar with the man that lives in that shanty about a half mile or so up the road from Clifford's place? Richard called him Jerome."

"Oh, yeah. The old hermit on the hill. A real loner." He scratched his chin. "Haven't seen him in awhile. He usually comes into town when his money gets low, does a little work here and there, then goes back to his shanty until he needs more. Never has caused any problems. Why do you ask?"

"Just curious." Hawkman stood. "Mind if I go to the jail and question those two bikers?"

"Not at all. If you find out anything of interest, let me know."

"What are their names?"

The detective thumbed through the papers on his desk. "The one with the bandaged shoulder is Jacob Broker, aka 'Chain'."

Hawkman raised a brow. "Yep, that fits."

"The other is Bryan Phillips, aka 'Brazen'. Both are on probation, so they're in deep trouble."

"Good, they'll be behind bars for awhile," Hawkman said, stepping toward the door. "I'll get back to you if I learn anything different."

Later, Hawkman emerged from the jail house, disgusted by the hour he'd spent with two of the lowest forms of sniveling human beings he'd seen in a long time. He threw the truck into gear, placed a toothpick between his teeth and clamped down hard. At times like this, a cigarette would taste great. On his way out to speak to Jerome, he thought about the biker who had the nerve to take the sweat-stained leather vest off his back and request Hawkman give it to Richard for the grief they'd caused him.

Pushing those thoughts from his mind, he turned up the road toward the Clifford place. A UPS truck passed him and he figured it had delivered the package from Uncle Joe. He still couldn't figure what the man thought he could send that would substitute for his actually being here in flesh and blood. Maybe Richard would show him.

Hawkman pulled up beside Jerome's old Ford pick up and started to get out, but an old black mangy dog, ran out from under the porch baring his fangs.

"Sit," Hawkman ordered. But the command meant nothing to that animal and he kept advancing, his hackles raised. Not wanting to battle the dog, he climbed back into the truck and honked the horn.

Jerome finally stepped out of the house, a big smirk across his face. "Yeah?"

"I'm Tom Casey, private investigator. I'm looking into the murder of Francine Clifford and would like to ask you some questions."

"Don't know nothin'. Weren't here." With that Jerome turned back inside, partially closing the door.

"Wait," Hawkman yelled. "Call off the damn dog and let me talk to you a few minutes."

Jerome poked his head out. "Don't know nothin' to tell ya."

"Maybe not about the murder, but maybe you could tell me something about the family."

"Don't know much."

Hawkman's patience began to dwindle. "Maybe you saw something or noticed some visitor at their place."

"Nope, didn't see no one. 'Cept that cop that kept comin' by. Never saw him stop, guess he was just cruisin'."

"You mean before Francine's murder or after?"

"Both. That's all I've seen. I've been out of town for a spell."

Hawkman exhaled and adjusted his leather cowboy hat. "Well, thanks for your help." He glanced down at the growling dog right outside his truck door. The dog hadn't left his stance. He even slammed the truck door, but the dog never moved.

Pulling back onto the road, he headed for the Clifford place. Why would Alberts be cruising way out here? That also bothered him. He'd have a talk with that man soon.

⟨‡⟩⟨※⟩⟨‡⟩⟨※⟩⟨‡⟩⟨※⟩⟨‡⟩

Richard couldn't believe the huge box delivered by the UPS truck. His heart pounded with excitement as he dragged it into the middle of the living room floor. He stared at the writing and ran his finger over the address. Yep, it was to him. It said so right there on the box, 'Richard Clifford'. Then he spotted the return. It just said, "Uncle Joe". His heart leaped with joy. Could the box contain his dad's guns? He quickly cut through the cardboard top with his knife.

Once he'd pulled the packing aside, he ran his hands fondly over the familiar cases. Opening them slowly, he caressed each gun. Uncle Joe had remembered and from their shiny looks, he'd taken excellent care of them. But why had he sent them now? Before he'd turned eighteen. Somehow, he must have found out about his mother's murder. He searched through the cases and finally found a note tucked underneath the Barretta pistol.

"Dear Richard,

I'm sorry I can't be there with you during this horrible time. Use these if you have to. I can't tell you where I am, but I care about you. One of these days we'll be together. All my love, Uncle Joe."

Richard wished he'd written more, but folded the note carefully and put it in his pocket. He wondered how his uncle had found out about his mom. Only two men had asked him about Uncle Joe: Zanker and Hawkman. Why didn't they tell him they'd found his uncle?

But Richard guessed his Uncle Joe was still in hiding. He remembered the threatening letters that used to come to the house. His dad had warned Richard that his uncle had a weak character and wasn't dependable. Shortly after that, Uncle Joe disappeared from the area.

When Richard examined the guns, he noticed how beautifully they'd been maintained. He realized the man had changed, maybe not fully, but for the better. That made him very happy. He wished he could see his uncle right now and give him a big hug.

Suddenly, out of the corner of his eye, Richard noticed the little light bulb above the door flash on and off. His dad had rigged up the signal so that his mom would know when someone came up the steps to the front door. He reached for the unloaded but threatening looking pistol.

# CHAPTER TEN

*Hawkman grabbed the leather vest from Chain off the seat and* flung it over his shoulder as he got out of the truck. When he reached Richard's entry, he felt at a loss. Usually the boy spotted him before he got to this point. So, how does one announce his arrival to a deaf person and not alarm him? He turned the knob and cautiously opened the door. His heart lurched. Richard sat in the middle of the floor, a pistol aimed at Hawkman's gut. Instantly he jumped to the side and flattened his back against the wall, praying the boy wouldn't pull the trigger.

Within a few seconds, Richard poked his head out with a sheepish grin. "Sorry, I didn't expect you." Grabbing Hawkman's arm, he pulled him inside and pointed at the boxes scattered across the floor. "Look! Uncle Joe sent dad's guns."

Hawkman stood in awe, his gaze drifting over the array. "How could your dad afford these? And why did your uncle have them?"

Richard explained the situation, then glanced up at Hawkman. "My Uncle Joe must have known about mom, or he wouldn't have sent them. Did you tell him?"

Hawkman nodded. "Yes."

Richard looked at him with pleading eyes. "Where is he?"

Hawkman studied the floor. "He asked me not to tell you. It's for your own sake."

An expression of disappointment crossed the boy's face and his shoulders drooped. "I understand. My dad told me about my uncle. Sometimes he gets into trouble."

Hawkman waved his arm over the boxes. "I'm sorry he didn't bring these in person."

"Me too."

Changing the subject, Hawkman knelt down and caressed the stock of the Barretta. "This is beautiful. Do you know how to use these weapons?"

"Oh yeah, dad taught me all about guns." Richard replaced the pistol into it's case and closed it. "I better put them away."

"What about ammunition?"

"It's in Mom's closet."

Hawkman remembered seeing the stack of boxes when he and Herb were searching for the papers on the house. In that flashing moment, he wondered why all the ammo when he hadn't seen any arms in the house. But the subject left his mind and he hadn't thought about it until this moment.

When Richard returned from his room, he pointed at Hawkman's shoulder. "What's that?"

Glancing down at his chest, Hawkman laughed. "Oh, I forgot about this." He handed the sweat stained leather vest to Richard and explained that one of the bikers wanted him to have it. "Of course, you don't have to accept this thing."

Richard took the garment and turned it over in his hands Hawkman noticed how closely he examined the brass buttons that decorated the edge. When he came to a space where one was missing, he rubbed his finger over the vacant area and frowned, his dark eyes narrowing into slits.

Hawkman touched his arm. "Is there a problem?"

The boy jumped as if in a trance and stuttered. "Oh, uh, nothing. I think I'll keep it."

On his way home, Hawkman wondered about Richard's reaction to the brass decorations on the biker's vest. Since he'd offered no explanation, he figured it had something to do with Francine's death. But what? He prayed he'd gain that boy's trust before he did anything foolish.

After Hawkman left, Richard proceeded with the chores and noticed Whitey waiting at the gate along with Old Betsy. The horse's ears were drawn back and his eyes had a wild scared look. Richard immediately glanced around the area, but saw nothing.

Occasionally, mountain lions and bear came down from the hills in search of food. He'd seen one of the big cats not too long ago along the edge of the property. Usually they didn't attack livestock, but it depended on their hunger. He didn't want to risk the chance of losing his horse and cow nor did he want them getting mauled. So after milking Betsy, he spread fresh hay on the floor of the barn, led the two animals inside and locked them up. He then made his way toward the chicken coop, leaving the full milk bucket on the porch as he passed the house.

There was a stillness in the air that made him wary. His gaze darted around the grounds searching for any sort of unusual movement. The chickens appeared restless and scurried about as if not happy with their normal roosting spot. The wire-screened windows of the coop were strong enough to hold out small varmints, but nothing as big as a hungry mountain lion. So Richard swung down the large, hinged wooden shutters from the top of the shed that were normally used in the winter time to keep out the cold and fastened them down tight. The chickens would just be a little warm tonight. Better than being eaten alive by a big hungry cat, he thought.

He withdrew the knife from the sheath on his belt and gripped it in the palm of his hand. The hairs on his arms bristled and his heart pounded as he sensed eyes watching him. His dad had always said, if you spot a mountain lion, don't break and run. Remain calm, breathe evenly and walk slowly. The minute you bolt, you're prey and that cat will be on you for its supper. But Richard felt his breath coming in ragged spurts as he started for the house.

Just as he turned the corner, suddenly, like a flash of light, the bucket of milk went over and Richard saw the large mountain lion sprang from the porch toward him. What he couldn't hear was the snarling scream of a hungry animal.

The cat knocked him down and the two rolled in the dirt. It took all of Richard's strength to hold the animal's head and exposed fangs away from his flesh with just one hand, since the arm with the knife had gotten pinned under his own body. He fought hard against the strength of the animal and felt the pain of the deadly claws rake down his back. Feeling adrenalin surge through his body, he thrust upward, rolling the animal onto its back. With his released hand, he plunged the knife with all the force he could muster into the cat's heart. Immediately, he felt the animal's body go limp as its life flowed away.

Yanking himself from the animal's clutches, he staggered backwards and stared at the bleeding trembling cat as it took its last breath. The damn thing must be five feet without counting the tail, he thought. And from what he felt during the struggle, he must weigh at least one hundred and fifty pounds. Richard's legs grew weak when he wondered how he'd survived that attack.

What he didn't realize was the scream of the cat had been heard for miles on that quiet night. Jerome had poked his head out the front door to listen, but didn't dare step outside, not knowing how close the animal might be. Even his dog had his tail between his legs and whined to be let in.

The sharp pains that streaked across Richard's back reminded him that the lion had left its mark. The skinning of the feline would have to wait until he cleaned his own wounds and stopped the bleeding. The hide would make a nice rug alongside his bed, especially to step on in the middle of a cold winter night. My, how Mom would have loved that luxury.

Feeling faint, Richard stumbled up the porch steps into the kitchen and plopped down on one of the chairs. Shivering, he removed the blood covered, shredded shirt and tossed it into the trash. He knew the wounds had to be taken care of immediately or they'd surely get infected. A poultice might even be in order.

He heated water on the stove and poured it into the bathtub. Thank goodness Dad had been wise enough to get a tub big enough for a man. He eased down into the warm water and grit his teeth to keep from screaming in pain. After a few minutes, he soaped a wash cloth and gently scrubbed the wounds. By the time he finished, the water had turned from clear to a crimson red. He couldn't see his injuries, but the hurt told him they were deep. Before he got too weak, he had to get back outside to skin the lion, or he'd lose the hide.

He draped a towel loosely around his back and reluctantly went into his mother's room so he could study the gashes in her mirror. There were four diagonal cuts. Two appeared fairly deep and oozed blood. The other two weren't as bad. He felt a bit light-headed, swaying as he tore an old white sheet into strips so he could tie a clean towel firmly against his back. Once he accomplished this, he put on a clean tee shirt to hold the make-shift bandage in place.

Going back outside, he didn't worry about encountering another mountain lion as these cats were loners and marked their territory. Another wouldn't venture into the area until all of this feline's scent had dissipated.

He had to skin the animal without stretching or tugging on the hide or the hair would fall out later causing thin or bald spots in the rug. Somehow, he managed to get the fur separated from the carcass without much trouble. However, he found himself completely exhausted as he lugged the heavy hide to the shed where his mom kept the large barrel and ingredients for tanning. He quickly mixed eight pounds of salt and four pounds of alum into eight gallons of water, then pushed the skin down into the pickling brine. It would stay there for three or four days before he had to do anything else.

He closed up the shed and went back to the remaining carcass. He grabbed the dead animal's head and dragged it away from the house toward the stream until his strength gave way. Figuring the remains would be eaten by other varmints within a day or two, he stumbled back toward the house. His energy completely spent, he dropped into bed and fell into a deep sleep.

The next morning, Richard awakened with a start. His eyes opened to see the policeman he didn't like looking down into his face.

"Boy, you okay? There's blood all over your bed."

Richard groaned as he tried to move. "I got clawed by a mountain lion last night. Lost lots of blood. I think I need help."

The officer's face turned ashen when he helped Richard to his feet and part of the bloody make-shift bandage fell across his arm exposing the deep gashes on the boy's back. He started to lift it off, but some of the sheet stuck to the wounds.

"Oh, my God!" Alberts exclaimed, turning to his partner. "Don't just stand there like an idiot, call for an ambulance. This here boy's hurt bad."

"No, I can't leave." Richard grabbed the cell phone from the box he used as a bed side table. His head swimming, he called Hawkman's number and counted under his breath. At eleven he left the message. "Mountain lion. I'm hurt. Chicken's need out. Betsy needs milking. Policeman called ambulance." Richard dropped the phone on the bed and swayed toward Alberts. When he grabbed the front of the officer's shirt to keep from falling, something shiny caught his eye. Alberts gently laid him back on the bed.

"You just lay quiet now, ya hear. Help will be here soon."

Richard stared at the man's crisp uniform, the light from the window bouncing off the brass buttons.

# CHAPTER ELEVEN

*When the phone rang during their breakfast, Hawkman and* Jennifer decided to let the answering machine pick up. But, as soon as Richard's unmistakable voice came over the speaker, telling about being attacked by a mountain lion, Hawkman dropped his coffee cup, grabbed his hat and charged out the door before Jennifer could speak. At that moment, the siren cranked up inside the fire station and echoed its alarming sound across the hills. Hawkman had already crossed the bridge and turned up Ager Beswick.

Speeding up the road, he kept questioning aloud, "What the hell would a policeman be doing at Richard's this early in the morning?" If there had been an emergency, the siren would have sounded long ago.

It took Hawkman less that twenty minutes to reach the house. He parked alongside the patrol car, leaped out of the truck and bounded up the stairs. When he charged into the living room, he found Alberts and his partner, Jim Perkins pacing. "Where's Richard?" he demanded.

Alberts pointed toward the bedroom.

Hawkman rushed into the room and stopped short at the sight of Richard tangled in a web of bloodied sheets. He squatted next to the bed and placed a gentle hand on the shoulder of the sleeping boy.

Richard's eyes flew open and a weak smile crossed his lips. "Hawkman, so glad to see you."

"What happened?"

Hawkman pulled up a homemade bench to the edge of the bed and listened as Richard recited the events of the night before. After hearing his story, Hawkman stood up and carefully pulled off the sheet, exposing Richard's back. He grimaced at the sight. "These wounds don't look good. We need to get you into the hospital as soon as possible." He knew that some of the deeper gashes would require stitches and it concerned him about the amount of blood Richard might have lost. "They might want to keep you overnight."

Richard's eyes grew wide and he shook his head. "No! Betsy needs milking right now and the chickens need to be let out." He struggled in pain, trying to get up. "I shut all the animals up tight, because I felt something dangerous lurking out there."

Hawkman pointed a finger at him. "You stay right there and quit moving around or you'll cause the bleeding to start up again. The ambulance is on its way. Don't worry, I'll take care of the chores."

"I owe you so much already, I'll never be able to pay you back," Richard said vehemently.

Hawkman got in his face. "Richard, I'm your friend. I don't expect any payment. The only thing I want is for you to get your back fixed. Now, get off it, will you?"

The sound of the distant siren caught Hawkman's attention. He motioned for Richard to stay put and he went into the living room. Hooking his thumbs into his back jeans pockets, he stared at the officers. "Alberts, what brought you out here so early?"

The officer shrugged. "Just cruisin'. When I didn't see any life around this place, sort of made me nervous after all that's happened." He rubbed the back of his neck. "So, we pulled in. That's when I discovered the horse and cow locked in the barn and the chickens still in their coop. I started searchin' for the boy. Finally found him here in the house in that bloody bed. We called for help when I saw how badly he was hurt. You think it's true a mountain lion got him?"

Hawkman's gaze had not left Albert's face. "Yes, from the marks on his back, I definitely believe it."

"What would make those cats come down where there's civilization? I'd think they'd be too scared."

"There's too many of them living in the hills. It makes for a real problem when they get hungry and can't find enough food. So, they come down and scout people's ranches."

Alberts' face turned ashen. "You mean they'll attack people?"

"Normally, they don't. But I have a feeling this one was mighty hungry."

"So you're saying we've got a man-eater roaming around these parts?"

"No, you're safe from this one. Richard killed it."

Alberts pointed a shaky finger toward the bedroom. "You mean that boy killed a mountain lion with his bare hands?"

Hawkman suppressed a grin. "Well, he had the help of his knife."

The officer slid into a chair, pulled a handkerchief from his back pocket and mopped his brow. "That's the bravest kid I've ever come across."

The ambulance came to a halt in front of the house and Hawkman met the paramedics at the door as they carried the gurney up the steps. He explained to them about the boy's deafness and what had happened. He also made sure they understood that he'd take care of the bill, then led them into the bedroom.

Once they had Richard strapped in and were moving him out, Hawkman patted the boy on the arm. "Now, I've got some chores to do, so I'll see you at the hospital in a little while."

Richard gave him a helpless wave.

When the emergency vehicle left, Hawkman turned to the officers. "Okay, Alberts. I'm going to ask you again. What's your interest in this boy?"

The officer stepped back, his eyes narrowing. "I don't know what you mean. I already told you we were just cruisin'."

"You're lying. I've talked with the station. No officer has orders to come this far unless there's an emergency. You're way off your beat and I've been told you've been doing this for some time. Even before Mrs. Clifford's death. I want to know why?"

Alberts stood up straight and sucked in his gut. "I don't have to answer to you. Who the hell are you to question my beat?"

Hawkman stepped closer. "Your territory doesn't extend out this far. I'm going to make sure your superiors hear about this, so get ready to answer to them."

The officer pushed past him and went out the door, followed by a sulking partner. "Well, good thing I happened by this morning," he scoffed over his shoulder. "Or that boy could have died in his bed." With that, the two marched down the steps to their patrol car.

Hawkman watched with disgust as the black and white sped down the road. He yanked his cell phone from his belt, called Jennifer and explained the situation. "Why don't you go on ahead to the hospital. Make sure Richard gets the treatment he needs and assure them that we'll take care of the bill. I'll be there as soon as I get through with the chores."

He then went into the kitchen, got the milk pail and headed out the back door for the barn. Betsy eyed him suspiciously until he put some grain into the manger. After he let the horse out, he took a deep breath and eyed Betsy's bulging bag. It had been a long time since he'd milked a cow. But damned if he'd let that stand in the way.

Plopping his butt down on the three legged stool, he took hold of the teats and smiled as he began to pump. Satisfied that he hadn't lost the touch, he gave the cat a squirt in the mouth and chuckled when it rolled over on its back and purred.

⊹⊱⊰⊹⊱⊰⊹⊱⊰⊹

Shortly after lunch, Hawkman and Jennifer stood at Richard's bedside. The boy had spent a grueling two hours getting his wounds cleaned, stitched and dressed. The doctor informed them that even though Richard had lost a lot of blood, a transfusion wouldn't be necessary. The boy was young and would rebuild his blood supply rapidly. However, he wanted to keep him overnight so they could monitor his condition.

Richard finally opened his eyes. "Damn mountain lion."

Hawkman laughed. "You're going to be okay. I'll take care of the chores as long as necessary. Betsy and I got along just fine. By the way, did you realize she's drying up? I only got a little over a gallon of milk from her this morning."

"Yeah, I know. It will be nice not having that chore, but I'm going to miss the milk and homemade butter."

"You could always let one of Zanker's bulls in," Hawkman said, winking.

Jennifer cuffed him on the shoulder. "He doesn't need to worry about a pregnant cow right now. She's getting too old anyway."

He laughed. "You're probably right." He turned toward Richard. We'll see you about eleven in the morning to take you home."

That evening Hawkman gathered the eggs, closed up the hen house and headed toward the stream where Richard had told him he'd dragged the cat's carcass after skinning it. He soon came upon the remains and studied the bone structure. Letting out a whistle, he commented out loud. "Big sucker." Heading back toward the house, he spotted Herb Zanker coming around the corner of the house "Herb, over here," he yelled, waving.

He hurried toward Hawkman. "Where's Richard?"

He led him to the lion's remains and related the story.

"My God, the boy could have been killed," Herb gasped, eyeing the size of the carcass. "That's a big cat."

"You're right. He's one brave, tough kid. I just hope it doesn't get him into trouble."

Herb furrowed his brows. "Why do you say that?"

"I don't think the boy's leveling with us."

"You've lost me."

Hawkman adjusted his hat. "Well, he's either found some clues or knows something. Has he mentioned anything to you?"

"Not a word. He's kept very quiet about the murder." Then Herb pulled a folded paper from his pocket and handed it to Hawkman. "Speaking of Francine, the coroner gave me a copy of the preliminary report. I don't know when the full details will be released."

"Anything we don't already know?" Hawkman asked, unfolding the sheet.

"She and the dog bled to death. He did note the cuts on her and the dog's neck were ragged. He figured the murder's knife had a nick in it that caught the flesh."

Hawkman rubbed his chin for a moment as he skimmed the paper. "Herb, don't tell the boy about this just yet." He handed the sheet back. "If I can just gain Richard's confidence, maybe I'll find out what he's hiding. This murderer sounds like a vicious son-of-a-bitch. I don't want Richard to encounter him alone."

Herb nodded. "When will he be home?"

"Tomorrow about noon. But I don't think he'll be up to doing his chores for a week or so. He's going to be one mighty sore pup."

"Anything I can do?"

"Thanks, Herb, but I think I've got everything under control."

"I'm sure Elsie's got dinner on, so I better get going." Herb waved and left in his truck.

Hawkman finished up and had his foot inside the cab of the 4X4 ready to climb aboard when the old Ford pick-up from up the road rattled into the driveway. Curious about what this man would want from Richard, Hawkman shut the door and sauntered toward the heap.

Jerome stuck his head out the window. "Where's Richard? Need to talk to him."

"What about?"

"I don't think that's any of your damned business," he said in a fuming voice. His face grew beet red as he huffed and puffed, struggling to get out of the truck. Once he had his feet planted on the ground he marched toward the house.

Hawkman stood patiently by. "Richard's not here. Want me to give him a message?"

Jerome stopped dead in his tracks and slowly turned. "What ya mean, he's not here. Where the hell is he?"

"He and a mountain lion tangled last night. Richard's in the hospital."

The man hurried toward Hawkman, his jowls flopping. "Is he okay?"

"Yeah, he's going to be fine, but the cat did quite a number on his back. He's got quite a few stitches."

Jerome rubbed a filthy hand across his face. "I heard the scream of a cat last night. Scared me and my dog."

"Well, this one won't be bothering people anymore. Richard killed it."

The hermit's eyes popped open. "He killed it bare-handed?"

"He used his knife."

Putting a hand to his cheek, Jerome's eyes glazed over as he headed for his truck, mumbling. "Oh my! That boy has got good with that knife."

Hawkman watched him leave, wondering what he meant by the comment. He'd make sure to ask Richard about it tomorrow. He didn't want the police getting hold of that type of information. Especially Alberts.

He thought about the deputy on his way home. The man seemed genuinely concerned about Richard's welfare. And Hawkman intended to find out what caused this change of attitude.

# CHAPTER TWELVE

*Richard found it impossible to sleep with three other patients* in his room, plus the traffic in the hospital hallway. He spent the first few hours of the night wide eyed and watching, until one of the nurses spotted him and made him take a pill. If he'd known it would put him to sleep, he'd have thrown it away. However, the next morning, he had to admit, he felt a little better. But, his back still hurt like hell and he found it hard to move without pain.

When Hawkman and Jennifer arrived to take him home, they found Richard sitting on the edge of the bed with a handful of prescription slips. A doctor stood over him explaining his limitations until the wounds healed. Richard kept nodding, but had a far-a-way look in his eyes. Jennifer introduced herself to the doctor who let out a breath of relief to see her and immediately repeated his instructions.

"I'd like to see him in about five days to remove the stitches." he told Jennifer, handing her the appointment card.

She glanced at the date and time. "This looks fine. Is there any permanent damage?"

"He'll have some scars, but no muscle or ligament damage that won't heal. He'll be sore and stiff for some time. But being young and healthy, he should recover with no problems."

She smiled. "That's good news. Because those injuries looked horrible."

"Yes, I agree that they appeared worse than they really were." He turned his attention to Richard. "See you in a few days." Then he patted his shoulder and left to continue his rounds.

Richard slid off the bed and grimaced. He took a deep breath and headed for the door. "Damn mountain lion."

Hawkman grinned as they followed him out of the room.

Jennifer stopped off at the pharmacy to get the prescriptions filled, then joined the two men in the truck. On the way home, she filled Richard in on the use of the antibiotics and how he only needed to use the pain pills when necessary. The boy nodded and tucked the pill containers into his pocket.

When they arrived at the house, Richard headed for the barn, checked the chickens and then the garden. Satisfied with his inspection, he lumbered into the house and wiped the sweat from his brow with the back of his hand. "Thanks, Hawkman. Everything looks fine. But I need one more favor?"

"What's that?"

"I've got the lion skin soaking in the pickling brine and now I need to clean the skin side. Do you know how to remove the flesh and junk?"

"Sure do. Done it many times. Where is it?"

Richard led him to the shed behind the house. Not wanting the boy to injure himself anymore, Hawkman pulled the hide from the large vat and carried it outside, where he washed it with soapy water and rinsed it with the hose. Jennifer helped him carry the heavy skin back to the shed where they spread it out on a large homemade table.

She turned to Richard. "Are you sure you're up to this?"

"Yes. It has to be done."

"So what are you going to make out of this?"

"A big rug to put beside my bed. Keep my feet from freezing in the winter."

"That's a great idea," she said.

Hawkman put his arm around Jennifer's shoulders. "This is going to take several hours. If you want to go on home, you can pick me up later."

"I think I'll do that. I'll return with dinner."

"Sounds like a good plan."

After she left, Hawkman and Richard sat down at the table and honed their knives on the whet stone. Hawkman glanced around the small room. "Boy, this place is stocked with everything you need to tan a hide."

"Yeah, Mom made sure dad and I had all the items we needed."

⚜⚜⚜⚜⚜⚜

Hawkman watched the skillful way Richard handled the blade as they removed the flesh, fat and tendons as well as the epidermal layer from the hide. He thought this would be the opportune time to question the boy.

"How did you learn to use that knife so skillfully?"

Richard took a breather, laid down the knife and stretched his fingers. "Several people have instructed me. My dad for one, even my Uncle Joe gave me some good pointers, but Jerome probably the most."

"You mean the 'hermit on the hill'?" Didn't think you knew him that well."

"He's a strange man. But when he'd come to visit and I'd be whittling or doing something with my pocketknife, he'd stop and show me how to hold it or how to move it over the wood. Just a few minutes here and there."

"I see. Where did he learn?"

"He told me the Indians taught him when he used to roam the hills. I wonder if he goes to see them ever now and then, because he leaves for long periods of times and no one knows where he goes."

"So, he's pretty good with a blade?"

Richard raised his brows. "Oh yeah. He can throw a knife and hit the bull's-eye almost every time."

"Does Jerome carry a knife?"

He nodded. "You can't see it. The sheath is hooked to his belt and he pushes it toward the back where it's hidden under that big coat. But, he showed it to me once. It's bigger than mine and sharp as a razor."

Hawkman pointed to the skin. "Did he show you how to do this job?"

Richard shook his head. "No, dad taught me how to skin an

animal and tan the hide. We started on a rabbit and worked up to a deer. We'd take the finished hides to the flea market. Got good prices for them too."

"Bet you did."

Hawkman noticed when the boy reached too far, he'd wince in pain. But he never complained and lifted the knife to avoid nicking the hide.

After several hours of cleaning, Hawkman helped Richard make a fresh batch of pickling mixture, then they shoved the skin down into the brine.

"The hide will have to soak for several weeks before it's ready to soften," Richard said, rinsing his hands in a bucket of fresh water.

The knowledge this boy had tucked away in his brain amazed Hawkman, but also worried him. He knew Richard had a plan to find the murderer, but he didn't have a clue as to what it might be.

They cleaned up the shed and Hawkman took the scrapings far from the house and dumped them, figuring the varmints would have them eaten before sun up. At the house, the two had just finished scrubbing their hands with soap when Jennifer pulled up in the van.

Richard started out the door, but Hawkman stopped him. "You've done enough for one day. Rest while I help Jennifer bring the food inside."

When Hawkman joined her at the rear of the van, she handed him a large basket filled with fried chicken and biscuits. "Did you guys get finished?"

"Yes. And it amazes me how skillful Richard is with that knife. He didn't nick that hide once. I saw pain register in his face several times on a long scrape, but he never complained."

"But he worries you, doesn't he?

"Yes."

She looked at him, a deep frown creasing her forehead. "You're not thinking he killed his mother and dog?"

Hawkman shook his head. "No! No! That never entered my mind. What I'm afraid of, is that he's going to attempt to find the killer on his own and use that knife, just like the murderer did to his mother. I've watched him sharpening it and seen the expression on his face. And before the mountain lion attack, I saw him throw it and hit the bull's-eye nine times out of ten. He's damned good. But, when he spotted me watching, he immediately put the knife away."

Her eyes wide, she grabbed his arm. "Do you think he knows who did it?"

"No, or he'd have already gone after him. But my gut tells me he's got some clues. This injury has put a kink into his plans. He's going to have to be in perfect condition before attempting anything."

Jennifer lifted a pot of baked beans from the back of the vehicle and started toward the house. "I can certainly see why you're concerned. Do you have any suspects in mind?"

"Yes, but I've got to do some background checking before I open my mouth."

"You won't even tell me?"

He smiled. "Not yet. In due time."

⟨⊹⟩⊹⟨⊹⟩⊹⟨⊹⟩⊹⟨⊹⟩

Once the stitches were removed from Richard's back, he felt great relief and began a ritual of exercises to strengthen his muscles. He knew he had to be in the best shape to continue his quest. Walking around the outside of the house, he searched the trees until he found a hefty limb jutting from one of the old oak trees. He tried it and found it supported his weight rather nicely. Using his arms, he slowly started pulling his body off the ground. Day by day, he made progress and before long could chin himself several times. It made his back sore at first, but as his muscles toughened, he felt the soreness leave. His everyday chores of working in the garden even helped. The increasing strength gave him confidence.

However, his mother's burial pitched him into gloom for several days. Despite the many beautiful flowers covering her grave, Richard's mind could only focus on that horrible scene of discovering her body. The memory of the fear he saw in her eyes would never leave him. It made him more determined than ever to find her killer.

After the funeral, the Zankers and Hawkman invited him to stay with them for a few days, but he refused them both. He needed to be at home in familiar surroundings so he could sort out his thoughts and let the ache of his losses diminish. They seemed to understand. The Zankers had the parting ritual at their home and afterwards, Herb gave the urn holding Ruffy's ashes to Richard.

It wasn't long before Richard found himself standing alone in his living room. He held the vessel of ashes tightly to his chest and fondly caressed it as he stood staring into space. Slowly, he walked outside and carried it into the field where the dog used to romp and play with Whitey and Old Betsy. Tears trickled down his cheeks as he removed the lid. He held the urn high in the air for a few moments, then turned it upside down and let the wind carry the ashes across the land.

He stood for several minutes, his heart aching. Then suddenly, a big wet nose nuzzled his back. He turned, dropped the urn and threw his arms around the neck of the big white horse. This animal seemed to sense Richard's needs and kneeled for him to mount. The boy and horse galloped to the Klamath River. He guided Whitey to the edge of a cliff where he stared out over the white water cascading over the rocks. Someday he'd raft this river, but first he had more important business to attend.

Using his knees, he gently turned the horse toward home. He felt a good run would be good for them both, so he gave the horse a gentle nudge in the flank. When the animal leaped forward, Richard grit his teeth and grabbed the horse's mane. The wind ruffled through his hair and cleansed his soul. When the horse stopped in front of the barn yard fence, Richard jumped down and opened the gate. Whitey followed him inside the barn where Richard wiped down his sweaty coat and gave him some oats.

After his chores were done, he went into the tanning shed to check the hide. The memory of his mother flooded his heart, thinking how she'd love having this rug beside her bed. He narrowed his eyes as he rubbed the furry hide with his fingers. Nothing would stop him from finding the murderer. Nothing!

Leaving the shed, he went to the house, fixed a hot dog, then went outside on the porch where he worked his knife lightly against the whet stone. It had become quite sharp and needed no honing, but he couldn't help himself. His mind went back through the day's events.

While at the Zanker's home, he'd approached Herb about the coroner's report. Zanker had hesitated, until he'd convinced him he had a right to see it, then he reluctantly handed it over. Richard shuddered thinking of the detailed description of the wounds on his mother and dog caused by the murderer's weapon. The killer had made a big mistake in using a defective knife. Now, he knew what to look for. No matter how long it took, he'd find the man with that knife.

He glanced up at the sky. There would be a new moon tonight and the hills would be cast in pitch blackness with no shadows. A perfect night for spying.

# CHAPTER THIRTEEN

*Richard lay on the couch in the living room with the lights off* and waited for the darkest part of the night. Even a cloud cover moving in aided him with his plan. He didn't fear falling asleep, for his insides tensed with excitement and his heart pounded. Finally, he arose, checked the knife and Pen Lite that hung from his belt, then pulled a navy blue hooded sweatshirt over his head. He went into the kitchen, slipped a couple of hot dogs and a left-over bone from a pot roast into a plastic bag. He didn't fear Midnight, Jerome's dog. The animal had always been friendly toward him. But, he didn't want a bunch of barking. And that dog always seemed to put on a big show of acting ferocious and brave around his master. Tonight, he wouldn't take any chances of a ruckus giving him away. Pushing the bag of goodies into his pocket, he left through the back door.

He started up the hill toward Jerome's shack, staying close to the trees, aware that Midnight would start carrying on as soon as he caught the scent of a stranger. Richard kept his eyes peeled for any movements so he could calm the animal as soon as possible. He didn't need shotgun pellets in his hide tonight.

His sight adjusted rapidly to the darkness and he suddenly spotted the dog charging toward him. You stupid mutt, he thought. If I were a bear or mountain lion you wouldn't have a chance coming at that speed. Richard whistled and called the canine's name. "Midnight, come here, boy." The animal came to an abrupt stop, his ears stood straight up and he started wagging his tail. "Come on, boy, see what I have for you," Richard coached, pitching his voice slightly above a whisper.

He waved the wiener in the air so the dog could smell the tidbit. Within seconds the mongrel ran to his side and snapped the meat from his hand. Richard gave thanks that he'd approached the shack up-wind and doubted Jerome heard Midnight's barks.

He didn't plan on entering the house tonight. That would come later. Right now, he just wanted to get a feel for the man, find out his habits, what he ate and drank. Most of this could be discovered by looking through the trash, that is, if Jerome hadn't burned for a few days. Most people in the hills had a metal barrel they filled with debris then set it afire to dispose of their trash. His luck held out. Fortunately, Jerome's container sat quite a distance from the house and Richard could use the small flashlight without fear of being spotted.

Wet garbage or table scraps were seldom thrown into these containers. Those would be tossed to the chickens or into the field for the varmints, birds and dogs. Unconcerned about the suet on the side, he rooted through the can and found many empty cheap whiskey bottles, a few newspapers and a large stack of magazines. When he flipped through the pages, he discovered to his horror that they were filled with lewd pictures of naked women and children. Some pages had even been ripped out. He wondered where they were.

Midnight stood at his side, his eyes pleading for more treats. Suddenly, Richard spotted the beam of a flashlight coming through Jerome's window. Dang! The hound must have barked for more tidbits. He flipped off his Pen Lite and quickly ducked behind the barrel. His breath caught in his throat when the beam of light momentarily stopped on the drum. Then he saw Midnight's ears stand straight up and he raced off toward the house. Richard breathed a sigh of relief. Jerome must have called him. Soon, the shanty grew dark again.

He didn't move for several minutes, then started to grab one of the magazines from the can before taking off, thinking there might be some identification on the front. But on second thought, he doubted Jerome would have that sort of filth delivered to his mailbox. He'd probably just buy or steal it from one of those adult stores in town. Anyway, he didn't want one of those trashy books in his house. What would Hawkman or Jennifer think if they saw it.

Treading his way back through the trees, he made it home without incident. Sitting down at the kitchen table with one of his old school notebooks, he wrote down what he already knew about Jerome, plus what he'd discovered tonight. A personality profile began to emerge of the man. Richard found it disgusting, but made himself withhold any judgment until he'd done a study of the other suspects. Then he'd make a decision.

❖❖❖❖❖❖❖

It had been over a week since Hawkman had requested a thorough background study of Frank Alberts and Joe Clifford. Kevin Louis, the retired policemen who helped Hawkman with his cases, usually did the work at the police station where he had access to their computers then would fax Hawkman the results.

When Hawkman entered his office that morning, the fax machine was humming. Not bothering to remove his leather cowboy hat, he poured himself a cup of coffee and crossed the room to watch the machine spit out the sheets. When it finally finished, he gathered the papers into one hand and went to his desk.

As he sorted through the material, he discovered most of it to be about Joseph David Clifford. Since Uncle Joe hadn't been in the area for months, he wasn't a suspect. But, he did take note that the man had been in trouble with the law most of his life. Nothing major, only minor infractions, but the report revealed he had a rough time following rules and regulations. It also explained Richard's comment about how he couldn't depend on his uncle. No violence appeared in the records and that eased Hawkman's mind in case Uncle Joe ever decided to come home and live with Richard. He found nothing in Joe's financial record that indicated he had any outstanding debt. So the loan from Alberts was obviously private and not recorded.

Frank Alberts' report revealed little new information. Hawkman leaned back in his chair and adjusted his eye patch. Taking a toothpick from his pocket, he stuck it between his lips as he scanned the top page. The documentation only went back a few years, starting with the man's career as a law officer. He appeared clean. It did catch his attention that Alberts' had been raised in this area and probably knew the territory better than he did. This made Hawkman curious and he decided to do more research on Frank Alberts' earlier life. He placed the reports in separate folders and filed them. He'd no more closed the cabinet than the phone rang.

"Tom Casey, Private Investigator."

"Hello, Mr. Casey. This is Joe Clifford, Richard's uncle."

Taken back by Joe's call so soon after reading his report, Hawkman cleared his throat. "Uh, yes, Mr. Clifford, what can I do for you?"

"First of all, do you know if Richard got my package?"

"Yes, he did. And it thrilled him to receive his father's guns."

Joe chuckled. "Thought that would make him happy."

"Of course, the boy wished you'd delivered them in person."

"I know, but I wrote him a note. He understands."

"I'm sure he's trying." Hawkman glanced at the ceiling, still not figuring how this man could abandon the boy. "You'd have no way of knowing about Richard's close call a few weeks ago."

"Oh yeah. What happened?"

"He got mauled by a mountain lion." Hawkman described the incident in detail, hoping it might stir up some compassion in the man to see his nephew.

"Wow, that's some brave kid. Glad he's okay. Well, I've got to go now. Just wanted you to know I've signed the papers in front of a notary making Mr. and Mrs. Herb Zanker guardians of Richard until he reaches age eighteen. I've returned them to the lawyer. I hope that's all it takes to put things in order for the boy."

"We'll keep you informed." Hawkman hung up with a heavy heart, thinking about Richard's lonely world.

He'd no more cradled the phone when it rang again. This time Jennifer's cheerful voice came over the line. "Hi, how's it going?"

"Bittersweet."

"Somehow that doesn't surprise me," she laughed. "I just wanted to tell you I'm going to run out to Richard's to return the washed laundry. He's probably needing his linens. Plus I purchased a few more groceries."

"We're going to have to be careful," Hawkman warned. "The boy is very independent and doesn't want a lot of charity."

"I realize that, so the things I bought are items he wouldn't buy himself."

Hawkman grinned, knowing that Richard had brought out that motherly instinct in Jennifer that she sorely missed since Sam had gone away to college. "Okay, I'll talk to you this evening when I get home."

⊹⊱⊱⊱⊱⊹

Jennifer rolled up in front of Richard's place in her van and proceeded to unload the items, surprised the boy hadn't come out to help her. On her way up the steps, she figured he'd greet her at the entry, but no one came. She managed with one hand to get inside and drop the freshly washed clothes and sheets onto the couch. After putting away the perishables in the refrigerator, she poked her head out the back door and noticed the tanning shed open.

Of course, she thought, hurrying toward the building. Jennifer briskly stepped inside and Richard jumped, almost falling off the stool he stood on as he reached above his head to smooth the hide he had draped over rods suspended from the ceiling.

He laughed. "You scared me."

"I'm sorry," Jennifer said. "Can I help?"

"No. Just about finished. Have to really watch the skin now, can't let it dry too fast."

She stood back and admired the fur. "That's going to make a beautiful rug."

He nodded and jumped down. "Thanks. What brings you out here today?"

They walked out of the shed together, and Richard closed the door.

"Brought back your laundry and a few groceries. I even brought a half-gallon of milk. I didn't know for sure how Betsy's producing."

"She's barely got enough milk for the cat now. But, you don't have to buy me any more groceries. Mr. Zanker talked to the owner of the old Snackenburg Stage Stop on Copco Lake. He's going to give me a job working with the horses. So I should have enough money coming in to buy all the things I need."

She patted him on the shoulder. "Congratulations. You'll enjoy working there. The new owners have really fixed the place up."

"Yeah, I can hardly wait."

"By the way, would you be interested in having another dog?"

He glanced at her and frowned. "I'm not sure. Ruffy was special and I don't know if another could take his place."

"None would," she said. "But I know of a family who will be having some pups soon and if you were interested, I'd let them know."

"I'll think about it."

Not quite ready to leave, she puttered around in the kitchen, and decided to put the remainder of the groceries away. When she reached down into the lower cabinet to make room for some of the items, her hand came upon a sack, which she immediately removed. Before she had a chance to open it, Richard snatched it from her hands, his eyes wide.

"Don't touch that."

Jennifer stared at him, shocked by his behavior. "What is it?"

"Poison." With that, he turned and walked out of the kitchen, carrying the bag.

She watched him go into his room and close the door. The item inside that sack felt like a large empty glass bottle. Why would he lie?

# CHAPTER FOURTEEN

*Jennifer returned home, bothered by Richard's strange behavior.* He'd remained in his room and didn't even come out to say goodbye or thank her for doing his laundry. Whatever he had in that paper sack, he definitely didn't want her to see.

She paced, wringing her hands, waiting for Hawkman to get home, but the minutes dragged like hours. Sitting at the computer, she couldn't concentrate on her writing and finally gave up. She decided the best way to calm her jangled nerves would be fishing, so she grabbed her pole and headed for the dock.

Her gaze traveled across the lake to the empty tree branch that extended over the water. It used to be Ossy's favorite spot to sit and watch her fish. She'd befriended the osprey years ago and she prayed nothing had happened to him. He'd been missing from his special limb for close to three weeks. Other osprey perched on the tops of the trees, but her whistle couldn't coax them down to retrieve fish like it did with Ossy. So, today only the sea gulls enjoyed the feast. Baiting her hook, she set aside her other worries and tried to focus on angling.

Fishing always did the trick and she concentrated on casting to the right spot for the big one. Soon, a double honk from the familiar 4X4 coming over the bridge caught her attention and she waved. She reeled in her line, rolled down the umbrella, collected her gear and hurried toward the house.

Hawkman no sooner hit the door than Jennifer placed a gin and tonic on the counter before him..

"Uh oh, what's going on? I haven't received this type of treatment in quite a spell," Hawkman said, chuckling.

"I've got to talk to you about something that happened at Richard's today." She proceeded to tell him the incident and he listened with interest.

"That definitely doesn't sound like him. He's obviously hiding whatever's in that sack. You say it felt like an empty bottle?"

"Yes. Large and very light weight. Do you think he's been drinking?"

"Well, he's definitely been through some trauma. I wouldn't think he'd spend his money on a bottle of booze though. But, who knows what a person might do under stress. And we mustn't forget he's a teenager, even though he looks like a mature man. He's liable to try anything and he has all the freedom in the world out there."

"You're right." She gnawed on her lower lip. "You know, another thing went through my mind."

"What's that?"

"Do you think that sack contained the clues he's talked about?"

Hawkman raised a brow. "You might have something there. He's never talked about the murderer to me or to Herb. I have this gut feeling he's going after the killer himself. And the only reason he'd do that is because he's found some sort of a lead."

"Now wait a minute." Jennifer sat down on the stool opposite Hawkman. "He's just a kid. Do you think he actually thinks that deeply?"

"Yes."

"Oh dear," she said, letting out a sigh. "Then we need to keep a closer eye on him. But how? He's so far away."

"I've thought about that." Hawkman said, chewing on a toothpick. "I need to dig deeper into Richard's mind. Ask some specific questions. Gain his confidence so he knows I'm on his side. Right now, I don't think he trusts anyone, not even Zanker. But, to do this I'll have to spend more time with him. I think the falcon might be the answer."

"It's understandable that he's a bit leery about you, but Herb's been around him for a long time."

"More than likely fear and revenge are playing a big part in his not confiding in either of us. He wants the first crack at the murderer and wants no interference."

Jeniffer nodded. "I see your point. Do you think there's anything I could do?"

"Just be your kind, motherly self. He needs that right now."

She smiled. "That, I can handle."

⟨⊹⟩⟨⊹⟩⟨⊹⟩⟨⊹⟩⟨⊹⟩

Richard hid the paper sack in his closet, then felt horrible about the way he'd acted toward Jennifer. Afraid to face her and embarrassed over his own behavior, he waited in his room, watching out the window until she left. Why had he responded so sharply? She looked so hurt when he snatched that sack from her hands. Why didn't he just tell her what he'd found? Of course, he knew he couldn't do that. He needed more time before he'd consider approaching anyone about the items. If the authorities matched the fingerprints, they'd arrest the suspect immediately and he'd never have a chance at the killer. That wouldn't do. The murderer had to suffer like his mom did. The Bible said, 'an eye for an eye, a tooth for a tooth'. And that's exactly what Richard intended to see accomplished. Even though he felt badly about the incident with Jennifer, he'd make it up to her later. Right now he couldn't let anything disrupt his plans.

Next week his job started at the old Snakenburg Stage Stop. He looked forward to working with beautiful horses and it would help keep his mind off other things. Also, he'd be able to buy gasoline for his motorcycle, which would afford him much needed transportation.

There were a few chores he wanted to get done before the job began. This afternoon, before the sun went down, he'd sight in the guns. He doubted they were off, but he'd waste a few rounds of precious ammunition to make sure. He couldn't afford not to be prepared.

How he missed Ruffy, who served as his ears and alerted him of anything or anyone approaching. Jennifer's offer of a puppy appealed to him, but he didn't have time to train one. Eventually, he'd get another dog, but for now, he'd have to rely on his own senses. He'd rig up a few more warning signals, like the light above the front door his dad had installed for mom. They weren't hard to do. One at the back door and a couple over the windows should do the trick.

Richard set to work and for the rest of the week, spent most of his free time accomplishing those tasks. He did take time to practice whipping his knife from the sheath and throwing it at the bull's-eye. He had the movement down so fast and smooth that if you blinked an eye you'd miss it.

By the weekend he'd finished his 'to do' list. He stood in the garden and leaned on the rake, surveying and admiring the neat garden where the vegetables were coming on in abundance. He glanced up at the house and grimaced. The next project; paint. But before that task could be accomplished, a killer had to be dealt with.

He shoved his hat back and wiped the sweat from his forehead with the back of his arm. Dragging the rake and hoe to the corner of the house, he stacked it with the other garden tools and went inside. His decision to clean off that brass button he'd found under the refrigerator bore on his mind. He had an idea on how he could save his mother's blood yet, still clean off the surface of the button so he could see the pattern.

Of course, he realized that his plan could prove moot. Not all buttons on a garment always matched, especially those worn by that motley cyclist bunch. They took pride in their leather, and the gift of the vest did make Richard doubt their guilt. He'd seen them flirt with his mother and how she'd rejected their advances. Maybe their harassing him was just a stupid child's game of getting back at her. They certainly didn't act like they knew she was dead.

Richard turned on the faucet over the kitchen sink and took a big drink of cool well water, then washed his face. After scrubbing his hands with soap, he went to his closet and removed the plastic sack with the button inside, careful not to touch the bottle's surface.

He found an old soft washcloth in the linen closet, wet it, then wiped off the top of the button until the pattern showed. Once he had the button clean, he sealed the cloth inside a plastic bag. The police might not be happy about him tampering with evidence, but at least he'd saved what he thought was his mother's blood. And with today's technology, he figured they could test it and make sure.

Sitting down at the kitchen table, he compared the button to the ones on the biker's vest. To his dismay, it didn't match anything. The ones on the vest depicted horoscope signs and the one Richard held in his hand looked more military or something that belonged on a uniform. He knew those biker's wouldn't display anything that represented authority or regiment on their clothing. Therefore, he ruled out that the bikers had ever been in his kitchen.

His shoulders slumped as he folded the garment and put it away in a drawer in his room. Then, he took the two plastic bags, one with the blood stained rag, the other with the button and tucked them behind the paper bag containing the empty whiskey bottle in his closet. One down and two suspects to go.

He checked the wall clock. Since he didn't have to milk Betsy any more, he'd have time to go to the river and catch a nice trout for dinner. The thought made his mouth water as he gathered his tackle. He stuck an apple in his pocket for Whitey, who always accompanied him in the field. They were inseparable.

Richard jumped on Whitey's back and rode to the river. The horse stayed at the top of the bank and grazed as Richard made his way down to the water. He kept a sharp eye out for rattlers sunning themselves on the warm boulders. A shedding snake is not to be fooled with.

He found a spot among the rocks where he planted his feet and cast into the rushing stream, then readied himself for a battle between fish and man, or so he hoped. It didn't take long before he felt a hard hit grab his hook. The fish took off down the churning water then jumped above the surface. Richard let out a cry of joy. He worked the line skillfully, letting the fish tire, then reeled in the eighteen inch trout and snagged him out of the water with the short handle net he had in his back pocket. Whistling on the way home, Richard laughed when he noticed Whitey flicking his ears. "What's the matter old boy? Does my tune hurt your ears?"

After cleaning the fish, he put it in a bowl of cold water from the well and slid it into the refrigerator. He still had to check on the lion's hide before he could concentrate on food. After examining the skin in the tanning shed, making sure it wasn't drying too fast, he headed for the hen house. He folded his tee shirt up to make a pocket and collected several eggs. Even though it was still light out, the chickens were ready to roost, so he closed up the coop for the night. He loved this time of evening. All the animals were content and it made him more relaxed.

He started for the house and noticed a column of dust rising from the road and hurried through the back door. After carefully placing the eggs in a bowl on the table, he dashed to the front window. His chest tightened when he recognized the black and white patrol car pulling up front.

# CHAPTER FIFTEEN

*When Deputy Sheriff Frank Alberts arrived at the station, he* discovered his partner had called in sick. That suited him fine. Now he'd have the route to himself, unless they'd assigned someone to accompany him. He'd been reprimanded by his superiors to stay within his territory so they might not trust him on his own. After signing in, he hurried to his car and drove away before anyone caught him. He could take care of the business at hand much better alone and wouldn't have to give any explanations.

Heading toward Copco Lake, he frowned, thinking about that private eye butting his nose into everything. He smirked. Wonder if they had the one-eyed joker in mind when they called them 'private eye' and not 'private eyes'. But then he shifted his position and twitched his nose. Best not underestimate that 'Hawk Man', or whatever he calls himself.

Alberts had questioned his colleagues about the private investigator and learned the guy used to be with the Agency. Obviously no slouch or someone you'd want to tangle with. That's when he decided to turn on the charm and act more interested in Richard's well being. The perfect opportunity arose when those lousy bikers cut up the boy's yard and garden with their motorcycles. It made acting concerned much easier because he couldn't tolerate that type of low-life anyway. He'd make sure those two stayed locked up for some time and out of his way.

He thought about Francine as he passed Copco Lake and continued on up Ager Beswick Road. Too bad she hadn't been more cooperative. Deaf or not, that woman was a looker. He certainly wouldn't have minded courting her if she'd have given him the chance. But, she kept her distance and that damn dog stayed at her side when Richard took off on his motorcycle rides. Animals didn't like him and he couldn't figure out why.

Alberts didn't like dealing with deaf people. He hated the way they had to look right into your face or eyes. Made him very uncomfortable. But, what infuriated him the most, worse than being cussed at, was when you'd be trying to communicate and they'd look away. You knew right away you were being ignored.

He rolled up in front of Richard's place and turned off the engine. Staring out the window for a moment, he fingered the long sheathed knife laying on the passenger seat. Finally, he opened the door, stood at the side of the car for a few seconds, adjusting his gun belt and smoothing down his shirt. He took a deep breath, threw back his shoulders and headed toward the front porch stairs.

⊹⊱⊰⊹⊱⊰⊹⊱⊰⊹

Richard had locked the dead bolt on the front entry and watched out the window for a few moments as Alberts strutted like a peacock. How he hated that man. His mother had laughingly told about how the deputy had visited her several times and made a complete ass out of himself. She knew his motive, all he wanted was information about Uncle Joe, but he pretended that his attentions were solely on her. She couldn't figure why he didn't just ask her directly, instead of playing such a silly game.

But Richard knew the man's interest was on his mother. He'd seen the lustful look in his eyes. That's why Alberts only visited when he spotted the motorcycle gone from the barn. Richard shivered at the thought. That kind of man didn't rank very high in his book. He thought him evil and not to be trusted.

When Alberts started toward the front door, Richard slipped out the back and headed around the corner of the house. Peeking around the edge he saw the deputy pounding on the door. He took his chance and raced toward the patrol car. Fortunately, the deputy had come alone which gave him the opportunity to check the inside of the black and white. He hauled opened the passenger side door and his eyes narrowed. There on the seat lay a sheathed knife. He grabbed it and dashed toward the back of the house, but Alberts spotted him.

"Hey, kid, what you got there?" he yelled, leaping off the porch in pursuit.

The deputy may have looked in bad shape, but he turned out to be more athletic than Richard figured. He made a flying dive and grabbed Richard's ankles forcing him to the ground. The officer whipped the boy onto his back and snatched the knife from his fingers. Richard tore at the man's shirt, deliberately ripping off a button.

Alberts straddled the boy's midsection, slid the knife from the sheath and twisted it so that the blade sparkled in the sun's rays. Smirking, he pointed the sharp end of the blade at Richard's throat. "What the hell you think you're doin', boy?"

Richard threw his hands up but the deputy touched the point to the soft flesh of his neck.

"Settle down."

Unable to move, the boy cried out, "Don't!"

"Whatsa matter, you don't like the treatment your mama got, huh?"

Suddenly, a firm hand clamped down on the deputy's shoulder. Alberts jerked his head around and found himself staring down the barrel of a Colt .45. He dropped the knife and immediately raised his hands. "Hey, take it easy. The kid just stole my knife out of the car."

Hawkman nudged him with the gun. "Get off the boy."

Alberts stood up with his hands raised. "Okay, okay. But you better sign to the kid, or whatever you have to say to a dummy, that it's against the law to take stuff from a police car."

Hawkman holstered his gun and in one swift movement, hauled off and socked Alberts in the jaw, sending him to his knees.

"What the hell you do that for?" Alberts whined, holding his face.

"If I ever hear you referring to this young man again as a dummy, a mute or any other name other than Richard, I'll make sure you don't get up."

"Okay! Okay!" Alberts said, staggering to his feet. "But you better explain what I said. I could arrest that uh...Richard."

"But you're not going to. You gave him a warning. That's all that's necessary. Now, get the hell out of here."

Alberts stumbled to his car, holding his jaw with one hand, slapping his hat against his thigh with the other. Richard staggered to his feet and watched the black and white speed down the dirt road, leaving a cloud of dust.

Hawkman turned to Richard. "You okay?"

The boy nodded then reached down and picked up the knife by the edge of the blade. Without touching the handle, he slid it inside the sheath and handed it to Hawkman. "I think the police should check this out. See if it's the knife that killed my mother."

Hawkman glanced toward the road, then back at Richard. "You have reason to believe that Alberts is the killer?"

Richard nodded.

"What makes you think that?"

"I can't tell you right now."

⁙⁙⁙⁙⁙

Hawkman watched Richard brush himself off, then turn and head for the tanning shed. He hesitated about following, not wanting to intrude on the boy's private world. But when Richard turned and walked backwards a few steps, waving for him to come on, Hawkman breathed a sigh of relief.

When they stepped inside the small building, Hawkman blinked a couple of times to adjust his sight to the dimness of the room. He stood in awe as Richard lifted the lion rug off the long table for him to inspect.

The boy had trimmed the edges and put on the first coat of Egg Albumin, water, Glycerin, pigment and preservative. Hawkman rubbed the hide gently between his hands. It had a wonderful softness that only the touch could reveal.

"You've done a beautiful job."

Richard's face glowed with satisfaction. "Thanks. If all goes well, I'll only have to do two more treatments, then it'll be done."

He put the rug back down on the table and stood for a second in thought. After taking a deep breath, he looked at Hawkman. "I want to show you something at the house."

Hawkman studied the boy's face for a moment and figured he'd made a decision to confide in him. "Okay, let me run out to the truck and check the falcon, then I'll be right up."

Richard looked at him, his eyes sparkling. "You have Pretty Girl in the truck?"

"Yes, that's the reason I happened by, because I thought you might like to go with me to further her training. Maybe even see if she'll work with you."

"Are you serious? I can put her on my arm?"

"Sure. Would you like that?"

Richard slapped his forehead. "Would I like that? Wow! Yes!"

Hawkman threw back his head and laughed.

They parted at the corner of the house. Hawkman headed for the 4X4 and Richard hurried into his room where he grabbed the brass button and the vest from his closet. He fished the button he'd pulled off Alberts' shirt from his pocket and compared it to the one he'd found under the refrigerator.

When Hawkman tried the front door, he found it bolted shut. He figured Richard had seen Alberts drive up. The boy sure didn't like that cop and he didn't know why. Maybe he'd shed some light on the cause soon.

Knowing it would do no good to pound on the door, Hawkman made his way around to the back and stepped into the silent kitchen. He wandered into the living room and figured Richard must be in the bathroom, but the door stood ajar.

He waited a few minutes, then gently pushed open Richard's bedroom door. The boy stood at the foot of his bed frozen to the spot, staring down at his open hands extended in front of him. Puzzled, Hawkman walked slowly toward him.

Richard looked up, his jaw taut. "They match"

"What are you talking about? What matches?"

Richard grabbed the leather vest from the closet shelf and brushed past him. Hawkman followed the boy into the kitchen and watched him place the biker's vest on the kitchen table along with two brass buttons.

Richard started rattling off the story about how he found the button under the refrigerator covered in what he assumed to be his mother's blood. He pointed to the two buttons. "The one I snatched off Alberts' shirt matches it," he said, in a trembling voice. "He killed my mother. Now, I'm going to kill him."

Hawkman took hold of the boy's trembling shoulders and gently shook him. "Hold on a minute, Richard. Those buttons are a dime a dozen. You have no proof that it came off the person's clothing that killed your mother. Don't go assuming anything or you're liable to end up in jail for life, or dead if you do something foolish."

Richard sat down on the chair and stared at the buttons. "There's one more I have to get. Then I'll know for sure."

Hawkman touched his shoulder. "You're not understanding what I'm telling you. Let me help you in your search. Don't get yourself into trouble. Your mother wouldn't want that."

Richard narrowed his eyes, jumped up and charged into his room, slamming the door.

Hawkman exhaled and hit the table with his fist. "Damn! I blew it."

# CHAPTER SIXTEEN

*Hawkman stood staring down at the two brass buttons on the* table. He fingered one, picked it up and examined it closer. The boy might have discovered something. But he couldn't let him know that just yet. It needed further investigation and he wanted to get more information out of the boy first. He sensed the strong dislike Richard had for Alberts. Had the man been involved with the family before Francine's murder?

Still staring at the round piece of brass, he raised a brow. Didn't he hear Richard say, 'he needed to get one more'? Did he mean another button? No question about it, he had to get back into the boy's good graces.

Placing the brass piece back on the table, he decided to take a chance. He went to the door of Richard's room and gently opened it, prepared to have it slammed in his face. The boy sat on the edge of the bed examining his knife. He glanced up.

Hawkman couldn't read the boy's expression, but had seen him throw that knife, so he stood ready to duck at any movement. Adjusting his hat, he cleared his throat. "Uh, I'm ready to take the falcon up on the hill. You still want to go?"

A slight sparkle of interest lit Richard's eyes. Knowing the boy needed to save face, he gave him a few seconds to respond then turned away. Before he made it to the front door, Richard appeared at his elbow. A surge of relief settled over Hawkman. Now, he'd watch his tongue with the boy and go at a slower pace, praying to regain the confidence he'd lost so quickly.

⊹⊱❈⊰⊹❈⊰⊹❈⊰⊹

Richard hurried to the truck, happy to be back in the big man's favor. He'd felt foolish when Hawkman pointed out those buttons were a dime a dozen. Why hadn't he thought about that? He remembered seeing them in packages at the store priced very cheaply and had at one time begged his mom to buy some. She'd refused, explaining that the metal cut the thread and that he'd lose them off his shirt faster than she could sew them on. How dumb of him to forget. But it still worried him finding one under the refrigerator, when he knew it definitely didn't come from his mother's sewing kit.

He climbed into the passenger side of the 4X4 and couldn't help feeling a bit intimidated as the falcon stared him in the face from her portable perch. "Will she nip me?" Richard asked, keeping his face out of her reach as he settled in the seat.

"Not unless you smell like a good dinner."

"What would that be to a falcon?"

Hawkman grinned. "Blood and guts."

Richard laughed aloud. He loved the macho talk. His dad used to tell his mom, 'Now, Francine, don't you get upset with this boy and me talking like this. It's man talk.' Mom would shake her head in disgust and leave the room. Then he and his dad would slap their thighs and have a good chuckle. Richard missed those times terribly and Hawkman helped fill that emptiness. He mustn't do anything to make this man angry again. With that decision made, Richard decided to tell Hawkman about Alberts. But he wouldn't mention Jerome for awhile. Jerome had indicated he'd been out of town at the time of his mother's murder and Richard needed more information before accusing an innocent man of such a deed. He needed more evidence on Alberts too, which reminded him of the knife.

When he jerked around in his seat to face Hawkman, Pretty Girl fluffed her feathers. Richard didn't hear her squawk, but sure saw her open that treacherous looking beak. He ducked, holding up his hands. "It's okay, girl." Keeping one eye on the bird, he shot a quick glance at Hawkman. "Will the police check the knife I took from the police car?"

Hawkman nodded. "I'll turn it over to Detective Williams. He'll see to it that the proper tests are run."

"Thanks."

They parked under a big shade tree and started walking up the hill. Richard loved the sight of Pretty Girl resting on the arm of the big man. Maybe one of these days he'd let him try.

When they reached the top, Hawkman glimpsed at Richard. "Do you know how to whistle?"

The boy nodded his head vigorously and let out a shrill sound through his teeth.

Startled, Hawkman stepped back. "You never cease to amaze me. How'd you learn to do that?"

He grinned. "Mom taught me."

Hawkman raised a brow. "Your mom?"

"Yep. She said if dad and I ever got separated that all I'd have to do is keep whistling until he found me."

"That's a great idea."

"My mom was a smart lady."

"I can see that."

Richard quickly changed the subject. because each time he spoke of his mother a lump formed in his throat. "If you want me to whistle a certain way, I'll have to put my hand on your throat and feel the air coming from your lips. Then you can help me when I practice."

Hawkman studied the boy in amazement. "Sounds like a good plan. I think we can manage that."

Richard watched with an eagle eye, not missing one movement Hawkman made with the hawk. After he released her, he turned to him. "Okay, come here and see if you can mock the whistle I use to coax her back."

The boy placed one hand on the front of Hawkman's neck and put his other in front of his mouth as the man whistled. They did this several times until Richard finally said. "Okay, let me try." After about the fourth time, he looked at Hawkman.

"You're almost there, do it again." On the fifth attempt, he gave him thumbs up and slid the leather glove over the boy's hand.

Richard felt butterflies in his stomach, wondering if the hawk would actually come down and rest on his arm. He stood on top of the knoll looking skyward, as Hawkman backed out of the way. Soon, he spotted the falcon and started whistling and calling her. "Come on, girl. Over here, girl."

His heart sank when she circled high above his head, then flew off toward a stand of trees. His sad gaze met Hawkman's, who instead of taking the glove, signaled him to keep trying and raise his arm higher. Richard followed the instructions and started whistling again. The bird flew from the trees and circled, but this time, she came down closer and closer. He feared his mouth would get so dry that he couldn't continue to whistle if she didn't hurry up and land. Then suddenly, she was on his arm. Her weight shocked him so that he had to brace his elbow with his other hand.

Hawkman grabbed the extra glove and slipped it on. He put his arm next to the falcon and she climbed aboard.

"Wow, she's heavy," Richard said, his eyes dancing with excitement.

"Yes, but you did quite well. You didn't frighten her at all."

Richard straightened his shoulders. "Do you think she'll do it again?"

"Sure, but not today. She's ready to go home now that her tummy's full. She has no more desire to hunt. We'll give it another go tomorrow, if you want."

"I'd like that."

❦❦❦❦❦

On the way back to the house, Hawkman encouraged Richard to talk to the falcon. The boy's voice tended to make the hawk nervous and he wanted her to get familiar with the strange monotone.

Richard turned toward him. "I know my voice makes Pretty Girl nervous. But hearing it should get her used to it. So if I talk to you, it will have the same affect."

The boy's reasoning never ceased to amaze Hawkman. "You're right. So what is it you want to talk about?"

"I'm sure you wonder why I hate Alberts."

"Didn't realize you hated him, but knew you definitely didn't like him."

Richard told Hawkman how the man had tried to court his mother. "She thought he did it only to get information about Uncle Joe. But he lusted after her. I saw it in his eyes."

"I see." Hawkman said thoughtfully. "Why did Alberts want to find your uncle?"

"I don't know. But mom saw right through him."

Hawkman pondered this for a moment. Joe Clifford never mentioned Frank Alberts, only Hal Jenkins. Were these two men in cahoots? "Did your folks ever mention the name, Hal Jenkins?

"Yeah. They said Uncle Joe owed him a lot of money."

"What does this Hal Jenkins look like?"

Richard shrugged. "Don't know. I never saw him."

"Did your folks know him?"

"I don't think so, but I'm not sure."

Hawkman let Richard out at the house and waved, assuring him he'd be back tomorrow.

On his way home, he thought about the things the boy had told him. The picture seemed to get more complicated as time went by.

When he arrived at the house, he put the falcon in the aviary and went into the kitchen to get a beer from the refrigerator. He'd just uncapped it when Jennifer came into the room.

"So how'd it go today."

Hawkman told her the story about the Deputy Sheriff.

"Oh, that reminds me. Kevin left a message for you to call him the minute you got home. He said he'd found some interesting information.

"Did he give you any clues?"

"Only that it was about Alberts."

# CHAPTER SEVENTEEN

*When Richard entered his house, he felt good about the excursion* with Hawkman and hoped it made up for his earlier stupid behavior. But he didn't have time to worry about that now, he had to make the butter. Removing the churn from the small pantry in the corner of the kitchen, he set to work. Within an hour, he had blobs of butter. The next step was to drain the buttermilk and collect the chunks into a chilled wooden bowl, then work it with his hands. After adding salt, he shaped it into the mold his mom always used and put it into the refrigerator. His mouth watered at the thought of smearing fresh butter on a piece of toast for breakfast.

By the time he'd cleaned up the mess and put everything away, night had fallen. Not looking forward to the excursion he'd planned, he slipped on his jacket, took the small flashlight from the pocked and flipped on the beam to make sure the batteries hadn't died. The light still strong, he returned it to his pocket and shoved a baggie full of hot dogs in beside it. He patted the cell phone and sheathed knife at his waist, making sure that they were securely attached to his belt before he went outside. Even though he couldn't see Jerome's place from his house, he stood for a moment staring in that direction. Somehow he'd have to sneak into the shanty tonight and steal that knife. He hoped that son-of-a-bitch hermit had consumed enough cheap whiskey to knock him out cold.

Richard paced nervously in his own yard. The thought of the

danger he might encounter kept him from heading across the field. Jerome normally carried his sheathed blade on his belt. Surely, he didn't sleep with that bundle wrapped around his fat middle. But what if he did? It could be a real problem trying to get it off of the big man. If Jerome woke up, he'd be dead meat for sure.

Hawkman had convinced him that the buttons weren't sufficient evidence. But, a knife with a nick in it would be worth looking into. He put his finger tips to his temples as an idea began to form. Smiling to himself, he breathed a sigh of relief. Maybe he wouldn't have to go to the hermit's after all. The new plan might just work.

He went back inside and returned the hot dogs to the refrigerator. Heck, he'd just as soon eat those than let that mangy Midnight have them. Shrugging out of his coat, he hung it on the peg by the door and headed for his bedroom. His mind more at ease than it had been in days, he fell into bed and slept.

Hawkman placed a call to Kevin, only to find he'd stepped out for a bite to eat and would return shortly. He stood around in the kitchen until Jennifer gently pushed him out of her way while she fixed something to eat. When she set a steak sandwich before him and headed for her computer, his gaze followed her.

"Aren't you going to join me?"

"No, I'm gaining weight and it's all in my butt."

Hawkman laughed. "You? You don't have an ounce of fat on your body."

Before she could comment, the phone rang and he picked it up. "Hey, Kevin heard you have some news about Alberts." He pulled a pad of paper toward him and took a few notes. "I'll be damned. That certainly explains a few things. Thanks a million, Kev, appreciate it." Hawkman studied his notes in silence while eating his sandwich

Jennifer finally glanced over her computer monitor. "Well, what did he have to say?"

He grinned. "What if I told you it's a secret?"

"Honey!" she pleaded. "You know I hate being kept in the dark about one of your cases."

"Boy, that's the truth." He glanced at her with a mischievous expression. "You just want to use them in your stories."

She smiled. "Well, I have to admit, I do get ideas." She left the computer and joined him at the bar. "Now come on, what'd he say about Alberts."

"Turns out, the name on Frank Alberts birth certificate is Hal Jenkins."

She leaned on her elbows, chin resting on her clenched hands. "Why would he change his name?"

"That's the juicy part."

"I'm listening."

"His dad murdered his mother."

"What!"

"After many years of being the son of a murderer, he decided it needed changing. So when Kevin found Alberts' name in the police file, he noticed it only went back to when he began his career as a police officer. That's when he decided to go to the public records and do more searching. He discovered Alberts used to live in this area. So it appears that when Joe Clifford approached Alberts about needing money, he loaned it to him under the name of Hal Jenkins."

"I don't follow you. Why would Alberts do that?"

"Not sure. Unless it happened to be laundered money."

"You think he's a dirty cop?"

Hawkman raised a brow. "You said that, I didn't. But, I have my suspicions. I noticed Alberts doesn't stay with a job long. Usually about a year, then he leaves with a flimsy excuse. It's very possible he's been taking bribes, then quits before he's caught."

Jennifer stood and threw back her shoulders. "I knew I didn't like him."

Hawkman waved a hand in the air. "Now don't go making judgments. I'm just talking. I'm not sure any of it's true. Only my observations. However, it just doesn't smell right. But, before I come to any conclusions, I'm going to talk with Uncle Joe, then I'll pay Alberts a visit when he's off duty."

"Good idea and don't forget to give that knife to Detective Williams. Richard just might have discovered something.

He snapped his fingers. "Thanks for reminding me. I'll do that first thing when I get into town."

Richard arose the next morning, his chest throbbing with excitement. He savored a piece of toast with the homemade butter, then attended his chores. When finished, he went to the wood pile and rummaged until he found the right piece of pine. He carried it inside the house and slid it into one of his old back-packs, then shoved a sports magazine in beside it. Clipping his knife and cell phone to his belt, he glanced at the clock. Seven o'clock. He wondered if Jerome would be up this early. Maybe he should give him an hour. After all, he had no livestock or chickens to attend. To make time move faster, Richard went to the tanning shed and applied the last coat of silicones to the grain surface of the lion hide. It looked beautiful. He ran his hands over the fur, feeling proud of his accomplishment.

Leaving the shed, he picked up the back pack from the porch, then dashed inside and grabbed the hot dogs from the refrigerator. He just didn't trust Midnight enough to go empty handed.

At the barn, he shoved on his helmet and started the motorcycle. He certainly liked his idea of facing Jerome during daylight hours much better than risking a dangerous visit to his shanty in the middle of the night.

When he reached the shack, Midnight ran out from under the porch as if to attack. But the offer of hot dogs settled the canine immediately. Richard glanced around and spotted Jerome coming from the out-house located at the back of the house. He waved and the big man approached him with a puzzled look.

"What you want, boy?"

Richard could tell by the man's expression that he wasn't too pleased to see him. So he quickly dropped the back-pack from his shoulders and fished out the magazine. He turned to the picture of a mountain lion and pointed to it, holding it up for Jerome to see. "I want to carve this out of wood, but I need your help."

The hermit looked pleased and scratched his greasy looking head. His expression softened as he took the magazine from Richard's hand. He squinted as he studied the picture. "Hmmm. This won't be easy."

Richard nervously pulled the piece of pine out of the pack. "Will this work?"

Jerome took the piece of wood and turned it over in his hand.

"Yeah, pine is good." He ambled over to his small porch and plopped down. He ran his finger around the outline of the mountain lion, then eye-balled the piece of wood. "Yeah, I think you can do it on this." Then he looked up at Richard, spat to one side and grinned, revealing chewing-tobacco brown teeth. "So you want a souvenir of the big cat?"

The boy smiled and nodded. "Yeah."

"Were you scared when he attacked?"

Richard nodded. "Very much."

Jerome grunted, then pulled the big knife from his sheath on his belt. Richard's heart skipped a beat.

"First we need to get this wood down to a workable size. How big do you want to make it?"

"As big as I can."

Richard had picked a piece of flawed wood on purpose and watched closely as Jerome's knife shaved across the surface. He prepared himself for the blade to hit the bad area.

"Shit! Jerome cursed, as the piece of wood splintered and broke in half. "You picked a bad piece of wood, boy. Gotta a soft spot in it."

Richard quickly gathered up the pieces. "I've got more at home. I'll go get them."

Jerome waved a huge hand. "Might as well throw those away. They ain't no good."

"I'll put them in my wood pile. I can burn it this winter. He jammed the pieces into his back-pack.

"Yeah. No sense in being wasteful."

Jerome heaved himself up off the step and slid his knife back into its sheath. "Look over the wood and make sure the grain is clean and even. Push around on it a bit. You'll be able to tell if it's good."

"Okay." Richard waved and jumped onto the cycle. He felt a thrill surge through his body as he bent into the wind heading home. Jerome had taken some long slashes with a full blade. There should be a pattern across the surface.

When he got home, he took the prized possessions into the house and stacked them on the kitchen table. He then ran out to the wood pile and picked up the pieces of pine he'd set aside. Knowing Jerome might be suspicious if he returned too soon, he made himself a sandwich and leisurely ate lunch. When he felt enough time had elapsed, he returned to Jerome's place.

"Took me awhile to go through and find the right pieces." He handed him two good sized logs. "I think these are better."

"Aah, yes," Jerome said, examining them. Then he held up one. "This will do nicely."

The two worked for several hours until the hermit finally heaved himself off the porch into a standing position and stretched. "Okay, boy. I think we've been at this long enough. My back's killing me and I need to go into town. Before you leave, let me give you some pointers on what size of blades you need for the smaller work." He found a stubby pencil, licked the lead, then searched through his pockets until he found an old receipt. After scribbling some numbers on the back, he handed it to Richard. "You work with a smaller knife for a few days. If you run into any problems, come see me."

"Thanks, Jerome. I'll do that. You've been a lot of help. Don't know when I'll see you again as I start my job in a day or two."

Jerome rubbed his big belly. "A job? Where?"

"Over at the Snackenburg Stage Stop."

He raised his brows. "So, you're going to shovel dung?"

Richard grinned. "No. I get to work with the horses."

"So they tell you." Jerome let out a belly roll laugh, then yawned and headed up the steps. "Well, good luck. Think I'll go have me a little nap before I go into town. Be sure and let me see that lion when you get through carving him." The man disappeared into his shack, slamming the door behind him.

Richard stared after Jerome. The man had not once invited him inside. What did he have hidden in there that he didn't want him to see? Dragging his eyes away from the door, he gently placed the wood piece into his pack and left.

# CHAPTER EIGHTEEN

*In case more information might surface, Hawkman waited a* couple of days, then called Joe Clifford one morning before going into town. "Hello, Mr. Clifford, this is Tom Casey."

"Oh, no, don't tell me I'm going to have to come back?"

"No. So far things are proceeding without problems. I just wanted to ask you a couple of questions."

"What about?"

"Do you know a Frank Alberts?"

"Yeah, he's the one who set me up for the loan with Hal Jenkins."

Hawkman hesitated for a moment. "I don't understand. They're one and the same man."

"What!"

"Hal Jenkins changed his name to Frank Alberts many years ago. Turns out he didn't like being linked to a murderer."

Joe gasped. "A murderer?"

"Yeah, his father killed his mother."

Several seconds of silence elapsed before Joe spoke. "I don't believe it."

"Did you ever meet Hal Jenkins?"

"No. But I talked to him on the phone. He certainly didn't sound like Alberts."

"He could have used a voice changer."

"A what?"

"Never mind, he probably knew some way to make his voice sound different."

"I don't understand why he'd tell me some other guy had the money, if he had it all along. Doesn't make any sense."

"I can't answer that. I'd hoped you'd be able to give me some clue. How long have you known Alberts?"

"I met him in a Montague bar about four years ago. He grew up in that area and fished a lot on the Klamath river. He told me he loved that yellow perch out of Copco Lake. I saw him several times after that."

"So, when did you borrow the money?"

"Before my brother, Bob, got sick. So it must have been about three years ago."

"Did you know Alberts worked on the police force down in Southern California?"

"Yeah, he told me he hated it down there and wanted to come back around the Klamath River area so he could hunt and fish. He really liked the outdoors."

"I see. Has he ever been out to the Clifford place?"

"Oh yeah. Lots of times. But when my brother started getting threats, he told me to get out. He didn't want his family being put in jeopardy because of my dumb actions."

"Did you tell Alberts about the threats?"

"No. I just got out as fast as I could. I was scared and didn't tell anyone where I'd gone. I just kept in touch with the family by a letter now and then from different places."

"So, you didn't come back for your brother's funeral?"

There was another pause of several seconds before Joe answered. "No," he whispered, then changed the subject. "So what should I do about this money thing?"

Hawkman's fingers tightened on the phone. "Right now, nothing!" He found the man right down repulsive. "I'll keep you informed if I want you to take action. Otherwise, stay where you are. I'm certainly not going to tell Alberts your location."

"Thanks, Mr. Casey."

He dropped the receiver onto the cradle and shuddered at Joe Clifford's self absorption. He then left for Yreka to check with

Detective Williams about Albert's knife. It had been at the lab for two days and he figured by now they'd run it through some preliminary tests. Maybe they'd found something.

The detective sat in his office mulling over the paperwork. "Hey, Williams, is that all you do?"

Williams shot him a look of daggers as he shuffled the sheets and put them to one side. "What brings you here today?"

"Just wondered if they found anything on Albert's knife."

"They discovered a slight nick in the blade and want to do some more testing. The nick isn't in the right spot to make the marks on the victims, but they want to do some more tests anyway. I haven't heard anymore."

Hawkman nodded. "When does the deputy report to work today?"

"Hold on a second, let me check." Williams opened his desk scheduler and ran his finger down the list. "Alberts comes in at noon."

"Thanks, Williams. I won't keep you from your work."

The detective grimaced. "Yeah, thanks for your thoughtfulness."

Hawkman left the station and headed for Alberts' place. The deputy didn't have to report to work for a couple of hours, so that should give him plenty of time to get information. When he pulled up outside the building, his inner sense kicked in. He glanced up at the second floor window and spotted Alberts looking down at his truck. Hawkman loosened the flap on his shoulder holster and got out. When he glanced back up at the window, the figure had disappeared. By the time he reached the entry, the deputy stood blocking the doorway.

"Yeah. So what do you want?"

"I think we need to talk."

"What about? I haven't been out to the damn boy's place in days."

"Not here to talk about Richard. I want to talk about Joe Clifford." Hawkman saw a flash of fear in the man's eyes.

Alberts shifted his feet and hooked a thumb in his front pants pocket. "You need to talk to Richard about him, not me."

"I don't think so, Hal."

The deputy stiffened. "What'd you call me?"

"Hal Jenkins, isn't that the handle you were born with?"

"How the hell you find that out?"

"I'm a private investigator, remember?"

Alberts ran a hand over his jaw and stepped aside. "Guess you better come in so we can talk."

Hawkman didn't trust the man and kept an eye on his every move.

◊-H-◊-H-◊-H-◊-H-◊

It bothered Alberts when anyone dug into his past, particularly this one-eyed pirate. How much did he know? "If you found out my birth name, then you know why I changed it. Ain't pleasant being a murderer's son."

"I understand that," Hawkman said. "And I have no question about why you did it. The thing that bothers me is why you loaned Joseph Clifford money under that name instead of Frank Alberts?"

Alberts jerked around and glared at Hawkman. "Don't know what you're talking about." Then he caught himself and took a breath. He felt his blood surge through his veins. Careful, he thought, maybe you can find out where that creep Joe is without giving yourself away.

"Come on, Alberts," Hawkman said, waving a hand in the air. "You loaned him a nice chunk of change and then he disappeared. You've been trying to hunt him down ever since. When you couldn't find him, you decided to try your charm on Francine after Bob died. But she wouldn't tell you. That made you mad, didn't it, Alberts?"

The deputy's eyes narrowed. "What are you saying?"

"Wouldn't that be a good reason to put a knife to her throat."

Albert's grabbed Hawkman's shirt and swung at him. But Hawkman blocked his arm and plowed a fist into his belly. Alberts went down groaning and holding his waist.

"You son-of-a-bitch. You ain't pinnin' her murder on me. I didn't kill Francine. But, you sure as hell oughta check into that deaf son of hers. He knows all about knives."

Hawkman rubbed his fist and glared at Alberts. "Yeah, well, the police lab is certainly interested in your blade." He turned and headed for the door.

Alberts struggled up from the floor and ran after Hawkman, grabbing his arm. "Whatta you mean, the lab is interested in my knife?"

Hawkman glanced down at Albert's hand and lifted it off his arm. "Richard turned it in for testing." With that, he walked out and slammed the door behind him.

Alberts slumped backwards into a chair and dropped his head into his hands. "I knew I should have left this place the first day I met that damned one-eyed Jack."

⊹⊱⊰⊱⊰⊱⊰⊹

After leaving Alberts' place, Hawkman wondered about the man's motives. One minute he's all for Richard, the next, trying to turn him into a murderer. He wasn't convinced that the deputy had anything to do with Francine's murder, even though the lab had found a nick on his knife. The man didn't have the stomach for that type of thing. He'd seen how Francine's dead body turned him green and made him sick. A seasoned officer should have more control. Hawkman couldn't visualize in his deepest imagination that Alberts had the guts to slit the dog's throat, let alone the woman's. He could see why Alberts and Joe Clifford got along. They reminded him of each other.

When he turned into the driveway at home, his heart lifted at seeing Sam's Toyota pick-up parked in front. He hurried inside. Sam met him and they hugged, pounding each other on the back like lost brothers.

Hawkman pushed him back by the shoulders and looked him over. "Good to see you, Sam. You look great."

"Thanks, Hawkman, so do you. School is terrific, but, boy, I've missed home."

Jennifer came into the kitchen smiling. "It would have been nice if this big lug had let me know what day he would be here. I don't have a thing defrosted for dinner."

Sam waved her off. "Don't worry about it. A peanut butter sandwich sounds great."

They all laughed.

"I'm glad I stopped by to get the falcon. I'm heading up to Richard's place. You want to come?"

"Whose?" Sam asked, his brows furrowed.

"I'll tell you all about it on the way." Hawkman went to the aviary and carried Pretty Girl out on his arm.

In the truck, he told Sam the story about Richard. Mid-way through, Sam interrupted. "Hey, I know that guy. We rode our motorcycles up in the hills together several times."

"Jennifer thought that might be the boy you spoke about. What's your take on him?" Hawkman asked

"Seemed okay. Don't know where he lived. We always met in the field and after riding around for several hours we'd go our separate ways.

"Did you see him often?"

Sam scratched his side burn. "Only about three or four times, but we always had fun. And I had no idea he was deaf. But now that I think about it, when we did talk, I always thought his voice sounded strange." He shook his head and frowned. "That's horrible that his dad died of cancer, then his mom and dog were murdered. Gives me the shivers. Who'd do such a thing?"

Hawkman shook his head and let out a sigh. "Don't know. Not much to go on either. But I believe Richard knows something, and I'm afraid he's going to confront the killer by himself."

Sam stared at him in astonishment. "Are you serious? Why won't he talk with you?"

"I wish I knew the answer. I'm trying to build up his confidence so he'll know that I'll do anything to help him." He pointed at the falcon. "He loves working with that bird."

Sam leaned back in the seat and looked thoughtfully out the window, his sandy hair whipping in the wind. After a few moments, he glanced at Hawkman with serious blue eyes. "Since I'll be home a few days, I'll ride up here on the motorcycle. Maybe if I get him alone, I can persuade him to confide in you."

"Thanks, Sam, I'd appreciate it." Hawkman turned onto the logging road toward Richard's place.

❖❖❖❖❖❖

Richard sat at the kitchen table studying the broken pieces of wood in front of him. Using a magnifying glass, he slowly examined where Jerome had sliced the knife through the wood. Engrossed in the pattern, he jumped when the light flickered over the kitchen window, indicating someone approaching the front door. He hurried to the living room, then breathed a sigh of relief when he glanced out and saw Hawkman coming up the steps. At first he didn't recognize the other person until he opened the door, then he broke into a big smile and pointed at Hawkman. "Don't tell me he's your dad."

Sam nodded and grinned. "Yep."

Richard hit his palm to his forehead. "I can't believe this and I don't even know your name."

"I didn't know yours either until just now." He extended his hand. "Call me Sam."

Richard repeated his name. "Sam. That's easy to remember." Then he turned to Hawkman. "How come you never told me about him?"

He shrugged. "Gee, I don't know. It just never came up."

"Where's he been?"

"School and working. He has a break for a few days."

"This is great! Maybe we can go for a bike ride."

"Sounds good," Sam said. "How about tomorrow?"

Richard snapped his fingers. "Oh, shoot. I start my new job. Would five o'clock be too late?"

Sam shook his head, "Heck no, it'll still be light out. I understand you'll be working the horses at the old stage stop."

"Yeah."

"Are you riding your bike to work?"

Richard nodded.

"Why don't I meet you out front of the horse ranch and we'll ride up here together?"

"Okay."

Hawkman started for the door. "Okay, boys, it's pretty warm out today. I don't want to leave the falcon in the truck too long. So come on, Richard, and show Sam how Pretty Girl likes you." He walked outside, the boys close at his heels.

Later that evening, after a fun day, Richard sat at the kitchen table under the single light bulb hanging from the ceiling, again examining the pieces of pine under the magnifying glass. The task left his eyes smarting as he studied each wood surface closely, trying to figure out any sort of a pattern or irregularity. The job turned out to be more difficult than he thought. The grain played tricks on his eyes. Just when he thought he'd spotted something, he'd turn the piece and the apparition would disappear.

He plopped back in the chair and rubbed his hands across his face. It would take sophisticated equipment to determine if a line from a nicked knife existed in the wood. Maybe if he got a closer look at Jerome's saber. But how the hell would he accomplish that? He couldn't ask him to pull out his big knife when the hermit specifically gave him instructions to use smaller blades on the more intricate cutting.

If he went back to him for help, he'd have to show that he'd actually done some work on the wood. But now he'd forgotten which sizes Jerome had suggested. He'd written them down on a piece of paper. Where did he put it?

He hurried to his room and searched the pants he'd worn that day, then remembered the sweatshirt. He crammed his hand into the pocket and let out a whistle of relief when his fingers folded around a small wadded piece of paper. Back at the kitchen table under the light, he tried to decipher the hermit's scribbling. He flattened the crinkled sheet with his hand, then turned it over to smooth it some more. But his hand stopped moving, for what he saw made him swallow hard and his heart race.

# CHAPTER NINETEEN

*The next morning, Hawkman made yet another trip into town* to talk with Detective Williams. Regardless of how good the local authorities were, he hated having to depend on them so much. While in the Agency, he could pursue his suspicions without having to answer to anyone. He pushed his hat back and exhaled loudly. But, he'd made that choice, so he'd follow the rules.

His intuition told him he needed to push Williams harder on this murder case. Or else, one of these days they might find Richard on that kitchen floor with his throat slit. A cold chill ran up Hawkman's back.

For the last couple of days, he'd observed Richard through his high powered binoculars, keeping far enough away so that the boy couldn't spot him. Since the day Zanker had shown Richard the coroner's report, the boy had pursued the search for a nicked knife. And it appeared he'd narrowed his suspects to Alberts and Jerome.

Hawkman still couldn't figure the motive for the senseless killing of Francine Clifford. The woman only had her son, a little piece of property and no money. He had a gut feeling she'd aggravated someone enough to kill her. But who and why? Yes, she'd been raped, but she'd fought tooth and nail. And the coroner couldn't make the determination if the violation had occurred before or after her death. Fortunately, that report had come in later, and Richard had only seen the part about the jagged cuts on his mother's and dog's neck. He suspected the boy knew his mother had been raped. That's why he changed her dress. He couldn't stand the thought of it being on her.

From the information Hawkman had pieced together from Richard, it appeared that Alberts had played a courting game with Francine. He tried to draw out information from her on the whereabouts of Joe Clifford, but it had back-fired. Alberts had a temper and a big ego that she more than likely bruised. But Hawkman doubted he'd slit her throat just because she shunned him. It just didn't fit Alberts' M.O.

Then there was Jerome. He told Richard he'd been out of town at the time of the murder. Maybe it was time to delve into that aspect of the case and find out for sure. Hawkman decided he needed to find out more about the hermit on the hill. What Hawkman had seen of the man, he believed he could well be capable of murder. And for some reason, Richard suspected Jerome.

But why would he kill Francine? He'd visited the family during Mr. Clifford's illness, bringing bounty from his land. That just didn't sound like a man with murder on his mind. The questions baffled Hawkman.

He parked in the police station lot and went inside. He found Detective Williams in his office, head bent low over his desk, engrossed in a stack of paperwork. Hawkman knocked softly. Williams lifted his eyes and grinned.

"Good, a visitor. I need a break from this damned paperwork. Sure could get a hell of a lot more done if I didn't have to fill out a report every time someone took a leak."

Hawkman chuckled and sat down in the chair next to the desk. "Anything new on the Clifford case?"

The detective reached for a sheet of paper. "Yeah, this just came. Alberts' knife does have a nick in it all right. But they're having a devil of a time trying to compare it to the wounds and question whether it could have actually caused the jagged cuts. Now mind you, they aren't ruling it out. They just have some doubts. So the report is pretty open."

Hawkman leaned forward, putting his elbows on the table. He looked the detective square in the eyes. "We need to move on this case."

Williams raised his brows. "Oh yeah? What's got your dandruff up?"

Hawkman told him about Richard's brass button search and now the nicked knife quest. "I'm afraid the boy plans on going after the killer alone."

Williams frowned. "He could get himself into a heap of trouble playing detective."

"I know. But my gut tells me he's bent on revenge. Sam's going to see if he can find out what Richard knows and try to convince him to talk to me. I just hope it works."

"When did Sam get home?"

"A few days ago. The boys were going to go riding a couple of days ago, but Richard got detained at his new job at the horse ranch and couldn't go, so they're going this evening."

"What do you suggest we do? I plan on bringing Alberts in and hammering him awhile."

"Have you questioned Jerome, the old hermit on the hill?"

"No. Thought Richard went up there, but didn't find him home. So figured he'd gone out of town."

"Well, he may not have been there when the boy went for help, but remember that turned out to be quite awhile after the murder. I think we need to question the man more and find out where he was that night. I've also been keeping an eye on Richard and spotted him up at Jerome's shanty."

"Oh, yeah. So what'd you find strange about that?"

"They were out in the front yard carving on wood."

Williams furrowed his brows. "You think that's odd?"

"Not really. The hermit taught Richard about wood carving and also how to throw a knife. But, I'm curious, because I got the impression that Richard didn't really care about the man one way or the other. So, for him to make a special effort to go up there and spend all that time gave me the feeling that he's fishing around."

"Hmm. Maybe we ought to pay this Jerome a visit."

"I think that might be a real good idea. But first, get a search warrant. It might prove interesting to see the inside of that shanty. Also, Richard told me Jerome carries a knife on his belt. Might be worth running that blade through the lab."

Williams nodded. "Okay, you've piqued my interest. It will take a day to get the warrant, so let's figure on running out there tomorrow. Think you can keep the boy in tow for another day?"

"Between Sam, the falcon, and his job, I think we can keep him busy during the day."

Williams stood and shrugged into his jacket. "What about nights? That could be the most dangerous."

"I've got a surveillance team in place and so far the boy hasn't gone out during the night." Hawkman got up, assuming the detective had an appointment or was giving him a polite signal to leave. "When do you plan on grilling Alberts?"

The detective checked his watch. "In ten minutes. Want to come along?"

"Wouldn't miss it."

The two men strolled down the hall toward the interrogation area. Williams directed Hawkman to the room next to where they'd be questioning Alberts. He'd be able to observe the procedure through a two-way mirror.

Hawkman stood to the side of glass and watched as Alberts entered next door.

His face locked in a solemn expression, Alberts gripped his hat with both hands as he approached the table where Williams sat. "Detective, what the hell is this all about?"

"Sit down, Frank. Just want to ask you a few questions."

Alberts pitched his hat on the table and scooted up a chair, raking the legs noisily across the floor. He plopped down and glared at Williams. "Sure don't appreciate this. Nobody's told me why I'm here."

"Settle down, Frank. This will only take a minute. You knew the Clifford family, right?"

Hawkman could see fear flash in Alberts' eyes. The man raised both his hands and immediately stood. "Hold it right there. I think I better get myself a lawyer."

"You don't need one yet." Williams said, motioning for him to sit back down. "I'm not going to read you your rights, I'm not recording and I'm not going to have you sign a confession. So just listen for a moment."

Alberts looked around nervously, pulled the chair back to the table and sat down. He put his elbows on the table and leaned forward toward the detective. "Look, I had nothing to do with her murder. I liked the nice lady and had no reason to harm her."

"I didn't say you did. But you carried a very suspicious knife in your patrol car."

"Hey, that deaf mute took my blade, then turned it over to that one-eyed Jack. How do I know it didn't get switched for another."

Williams narrowed his eyes. "Your fingerprints were all over the handle."

Alberts immediately deflated and Hawkman watched the fear creep back into his face.

The detective waved a piece of paper he held in his hand. "I've checked the scheduling record for June second, the date of Francine's death. You were seen in the Copco Lake area. It so happens, your partner Jim Perkins had a doctor's appointment and didn't accompany you. I'm giving you forty-eight hours to document every hour of that day. If you can't account for the time, then you better consider getting a lawyer." Williams stood up and straightened his coat. "I'd get started if I were you." With those words, the detective left the room.

Alberts stared at the door for a few seconds, then snatched his hat from the table and stormed out of the room.

Hawkman waited a few minutes before joining Williams in his office. "The man's scared."

"Yeah, I know."

"You think he did it?" Hawkman asked.

"Hard to say. He's got a temper, but nowhere in his record is there a history of violence. Even though his father died in prison after being convicted of killing Alberts' mother."

"So you know about his past?"

Williams nodded. "Had to do some research on the man, because too many complaints were coming in about his crude behavior. Even his partner doesn't want to hang with him."

Hawkman then related his conversation with Joe Clifford.

"Where the hell is Richard's uncle, anyway?"

"Can't get him to come back. He's afraid of someone he's indebted to."

"Richard could certainly use his support. You realize the boy is a suspect."

The words hit Hawkman like a bolt of lightening. "Williams, you can't believe for a minute that boy killed his mother?"

"I can't go on my beliefs. You know that. It's the facts I have to build a case on, and that boy has no alibi. I want his knife. If you can get it, all the better. Otherwise, I'll have to confiscate it. I'm going in to search his house at the same time I go to Jerome's, which will more than likely be tomorrow.

Hawkman felt the blood drain from his face. "Give me another day. Give Sam a chance to talk to Richard before you invade his privacy. At least give me a chance to talk to the boy."

Williams glared at him. "You're the one who wanted me to move fast."

"I do, I do. But to find the killer. You and I both know it's not Richard."

The detective walked over to the window and stared out. Rubbing his fingers over the stubble on his chin, he turned. "Okay, I'm going to give you three days. But I'm going up to that hermit's place in the morning. You're welcome to join me. Be there at nine."

Hawkman breathed a sigh of relief. "Thanks. I'll be there. And I owe you one."

# CHAPTER TWENTY

*Leaving the police station, Hawkman continued on to his office* in Medford. It dismayed him to think Williams even considered Richard a suspect. But he could see the logic behind it. No clues, no witnesses, Richard skilled with a knife and the only one around. He shuddered putting himself into the boy's shoes. Years ago no one would have ever considered a kid killing his mother. But today morals and respect have gone down the tubes.

He grabbed a donut from the shop, then climbed the stairs to his office. When he opened the door, a blast of hot air hit him in the face. He immediately opened the windows and turned on the air conditioner. After a few minutes, the room cooled considerably.

He tossed his hat on top of the coat rack and checked the fax machine. No messages appeared on the phone, so he sat down at the desk and booted up the computer. He opened the file on the Clifford murder and stared at the few reports inside.

Unfortunately, by the time the police were called into the case, any pertinent clues were long gone. They'd combed the area around Richard's house and found nothing unusual. When they dusted for prints in the kitchen where the murder had taken place, the fingerprints had been obliterated by Richard's scrubbing. The only ones the technicians found belonged to Richard or his mother.

Hawkman kept thinking about the sack Jennifer found under the cabinet that Richard had snatched away from her. His unusual rude behavior indicated it definitely contained something he didn't want her to see. Jennifer felt certain the sack held a glass bottle.

If Richard had found, say an empty whiskey bottle outside, it just might have prints on it. Is that what he's hiding? Possibly, since he'd seen no evidence that Richard had been drinking on his own. And Jennifer found no liquor in the cabinets while putting away groceries, not even wine. Evidently, the Cliffords weren't drinkers.

Considering Richard's naive way of thinking, he'd want to hide the evidence from the police until he'd found the murderer and taken revenge. Dear God, didn't the kid realize he could get himself killed?

Hawkman remembered the day he went into Richard's house after they returned from working with Pretty Girl. Pieces of pine lay on the kitchen table that looked like they'd been sliced with a knife. Richard had been to Jerome's the day before, carving outside. Why would he keep extra pieces of ruined wood? He hadn't thought much about it at the moment. Richard always had that knife out, whittling something.

But there was something else on that table that caught his attention for a split second. What the hell was it? He couldn't remember. Closing his eyes, he tried to recall the surface of the table and why it struck him strange. Then he bolted up right in his chair. A magnifying glass! He'd been checking the pattern in the wood. Somehow Richard had gotten Jerome to slice through that wood.

Hawkman rubbed his hand across the stubble on his chin. There's no way in hell the boy could detect a pattern in a piece of wood with a store-bought magnifying glass. Did Jerome have any suspicion of the boy's intentions? Goose bumps rose on his arms.

Two of his men working the night shift, reported that neither Jerome nor Richard were seen out at night or had behaved in an unusual way. Maybe Richard had given up. He shook his head. No, that's dreaming. That boy won't give up. The drive for revenge is too powerful. Richard had something else up his sleeve. He sucked in a deep breath and stared into space. I hope you're having some luck, Sam, he prayed silently.

Sam and Richard climbed up the steep grade on their cycles then stopped at the crest to look over the white water of the Klamath river churning below. Sam wondered when the moment would come that he could approach Richard about the murder. He hated to spoil the good time both were having, but he knew he wouldn't have another opportunity, because he had to return to school tomorrow.

Straddling the bike, he took off his helmet and hung it on the handlebars, then took his water container and flipped it open. After taking a big gulp, he wiped his mouth with the back of his hand and offered it to Richard. He waved him off and showed him he had his own. Sam threw his leg over the bike and kicked down the stand. Richard did the same. The two boys walked toward the shade of a nearby tree and sat down on a fallen log.

Making sure he faced Richard, Sam spoke. "This is sure beautiful country. I really miss it when I'm at school."

"Do you like college?" Richard asked.

Sam nodded. "Yeah, a lot. Do you plan on going?"

Richard shrugged. "I can't afford it."

"You could get financial aid."

"I can't leave the place. Everything would die."

Richard looked over the vast area with a faraway look in his eyes. Then he quickly turned his eyes back on Sam. "My mom always talked about when I'd go to college."

"I'm really sorry about your parents," Sam said. "It doesn't seem fair that you lost them both in such a short time."

"I'll make sure the murderer pays."

"How?" Sam asked. "You can't find a killer by yourself."

"I think I know who did it. I just have to get the proof."

"Hey, that's dangerous. You could get yourself killed. If you know something, you ought to talk to Hawkman. He's trained to hunt down killers and that kind of stuff."

Richard stood, his expression concerned. He started pacing in front of Sam, kicking up fine dust with his boots. "Yeah, I know. I've thought about it. But he'd probably think me crazy."

"No way. He's a really neat guy."

Then Richard looked at him, puzzled. "You said he's your dad. Why don't you call him dad?"

"Because he and Jennifer adopted me. My parents were killed and I had no relatives to look after me."

Richard stared at him wide eyed. "Your parents were killed?"

Sam raised his hand. "Not murdered. They were in an automobile accident."

Richard let out a sigh. "But you still lost them."

"Yeah. It was hard."

The boy nodded. "But you trust Hawkman. He's been a good dad?"

"The best. And he really likes you. He wants to help, but you won't let him."

Richard bit his lower lip. "I'm not used to having people around, snooping into my personal affairs. I didn't go to public school."

"Really," Sam said. "How'd you get so smart?"

"My mom. She taught me how to read, speak with my voice, do math and other subjects. I know a lot of stuff."

"I realize that and have no doubt you'd make it in college. What grade would you be in now?"

"I'd probably be graduating from high school this coming year, if my mom were still alive."

"Why don't you enroll in the high school here so you can get your diploma? Jennifer would help you."

Richard kicked at a pebble on the ground and sent it flying through the air. "I can't expect people to help me. I need to do these things on my own. I have to learn to be self-sufficient."

Sam felt he might be losing Richard and took him by the arm. "We all need people. You need to get that through your head. There are some things we can't do alone. You need Hawkman right now and I really hope you get his help before you get into trouble."

Richard stared into Sam's face. "You really believe that, don't you?"

"Yes."

"But we're different, Sam. I'm deaf. I've been taught all my life to depend on myself for my needs. I don't want anyone's sympathy."

"Look, Richard. You've already proved yourself with Hawkman. He knows you're smart and he knows you're very independent. That's why he's holding back. If you were some whimpering kid, he and Zanker would have let the Child Services come in and take over. But they didn't. They didn't want to ruin the pride they saw in you. Give him a chance."

Richard started back toward the motorcycle. Sam let out a long sigh, wondering if he'd made any headway with the stubborn and independent mind of Richard Clifford. Sam strolled back to his bike and glanced at Richard who had his hand on the starter. The boy turned toward him.

"Thanks, Sam. I'm going to really think about what you said."

With that, his cycle engine roared to life. He put the bike into gear and started down the hill, the back wheel kicking out pebbles in it's wake.

Sam watched him, his heart aching for the lonely young man. "Let Hawkman help you," he whispered, as he followed Richard down the hill.

⫟⊹⊹⊹⊹⫟

Hawkman arrived home early, went straight to the dining room window and stood staring out towards Richard's place.

Jennifer slid her arm around his waist. "What's troubling you?"

"Detective Williams told me today that Richard's a suspect in the murder of his mother."

"You had to realize that was coming."

"I know. I just didn't want to think about it. I'm just praying that Sam had some luck in convincing Richard to confide in me."

"He'll do all he can."

"I think I'm going to drive up there."

"You want me to come?"

"No, not this time. Maybe if it's just Sam and me, he'll talk.,"

She raised up on her tiptoes and kissed his cheek. "Good luck. I hope Richard comes to his senses."

Hawkman hugged her and left.

The boys weren't back when Hawkman arrived at Richard's place. He sat down on the porch steps to wait. The sun dipped low in the horizon before he heard the distinct sound of motorcycles and saw the dirt cloud in the distance. The boys soon pulled up, Richard veering off toward the barn as Sam came to a halt behind Hawkman's 4X4.

"You guys have a good ride?" Hawkman called out.

Sam pulled off his helmet and slid his gloves inside, before joining him on the steps. "Yeah, it's great out there."

"Any luck?" Hawkman asked quickly, before Richard came in sight.

Sam let out a sigh. "I tried. I don't know how much good I did. But I really tried.

Hawkman patted him on the back. "I'm sure you did all you could."

Richard soon strolled around the corner of the house.

"Hi, Hawkman. I hope you weren't worried."

"Not at all. Just thought I drive out and talk to you. I have something to tell you."

Richard stared at Hawkman for a moment. "It's not good news, is it?"

He shook his head. "I'm afraid not, son. We have three days to find the killer. If we don't find him, the police will more than likely arrest you for the murder of your mother."

# CHAPTER TWENTY ONE

*Richard felt his chest tighten as he absorbed what Hawkman* had just said.

He stared at the man he so admired. "What am I going to do? You can't let them arrest me. You know I didn't hurt my mom."

Hawkman's shoulders drooped as he exhaled. "And I know the police are going to want to check your knife."

Richard immediately pulled it off his belt and held it out to Hawkman. "They can have it. In fact, I want them to check it out so they'll know this isn't the knife that killed her."

"Wait and give it to them later." Hawkman looked into Richard's eyes.

"Do you know whose knife did?"

The boy turned his eyes downward and scuffed his boot against the hard pan ground. "I have my suspicions."

"Why won't you tell me?"

Richard hesitated for a moment. "Tomorrow. I promise I'll tell you then."

Hawkman stood and glanced down at the boy. "I'll be here first thing in the morning. Don't do anything stupid tonight."

He nodded. "Okay."

Motioning for Sam to follow, Hawkman headed for the truck.

Sam patted Richard on the shoulder. "See ya in about three months, buddy."

He looked surprised. "How come so long?"

"I won't get another vacation until then." Sam waved, then jogged toward the cycle. He pushed on his helmet, hooked the strap under his chin and put on his gloves. By the time he started down the driveway, Hawkman had traveled half-way down the logging road.

Richard watched the vehicles disappear and the dust settle before he thrust his hands deep into his front jeans pockets and stared at the ground. Then he angrily kicked a rock, sending it skidding across the dirt. Had that damned Deputy Sheriff Alberts decided to arrest him? Hawkman hadn't mentioned any report about the officer's knife. But it stood to reason, if they'd decided to arrest him instead, Alberts' knife must have come out clean.

He recalled one of Alberts' visits when his mother was still alive. He'd returned from his motorcycle ride early because the cycle had been cutting out and he needed to make some minor adjustments. When he'd finished working on the bike, he delayed going inside so he wouldn't have to listen to Alberts' stupid remarks. He set up a target in the barnyard and practiced throwing his knife. Suddenly, Alberts charged out of the house, his hands protecting his head. Seconds later, his hat came flying from the doorway, bouncing off his back.

Richard remembered chuckling to himself, figuring his mother had gotten rid of the officer again. Did the man have such a thick head that he couldn't get the picture that she wanted nothing to do with him? Thinking Alberts had left, he continued throwing his knife. He jumped when he realized Alberts was standing beside him, holding his blade. He challenged him to a game of who could hit the bull's-eye the most.

After about ten pitches, Richard hit the target seven out of ten times while Alberts never even got close. The deputy turned on his heel and stormed to his car. Richard knew it infuriated him to be shown up by a kid. A deaf dummy at that, as he called him. How he hated that man.

He took a deep breath and started up the steps. He didn't like Alberts and wasn't afraid of him. But Jerome, was another story. That man scared the hell out of him.

Regardless of how frightened he felt, he had to push ahead with his plan. The carving idea had to be dropped, since there wouldn't be time. He'd promised Hawkman he'd tell him who he suspected tomorrow and he wanted to make sure, without a doubt, that he told him the right one. And he could bet his bottom dollar that Hawkman would be here first thing in the morning, just like he'd promised.

۞۞۞۞۞۞

On the ride home, Hawkman thought about how shocked Richard looked when he told him he might be arrested. He slapped his hand against the steering wheel. "There's no way in hell I'll let that happen," he said aloud, then glanced into the rear view mirror at Sam as he rode his bike a few yards behind him.

After pulling up into the driveway at home, Hawkman didn't wait for Sam. He hopped out of his truck and headed inside. Brushing past Jennifer, he went straight to the phone. First he called Williams and told him if he got a dispatch from him this evening, to send back up to the Clifford place. Then he called Kevin and Stan, the two retired officers taking nightly turns watching Richard to notify them that he'd take the duty tonight. When he dropped the receiver into the cradle, he glanced up to see Jennifer facing him with her hands on her hips.

"May I ask what that was all about?"

At that moment, Sam ran in, grabbed a Coke from the refrigerator and leaned against the counter. "So what'd I miss?"

Hawkman grinned at his son, then explained to Jennifer what he'd told Richard. "I got the impression the boy's going to visit Jerome's place tonight. And that worries me."

"You should have kept Kevin and Stan on duty. Now you'll be out there alone. What if you need help?"

"I've alerted Williams. But my objective is to prevent Richard from ever leaving his place. I'm hoping there won't be any confrontation with Jerome. That's Williams' job and he'll be doing that tomorrow."

Jennifer gnawed on her lower lip. "I don't like it. From what you've told me about that man, he could be dangerous."

"Just because a guy wears dirty clothes and is gruesome looking, doesn't make him dangerous. He did show some compassion during Mr. Clifford's illness. And, he certainly showed patience while teaching the boy how to carve. There's no evidence that he's violent or worse, a killer. He's been around this area for years and never caused a problem."

She hugged herself. "I know. I just have these bad vibes about you being out there alone."

"I'll go with him," Sam intervened.

Jennifer whirled around and glared at him. "No way! You have that long drive ahead of you tomorrow and need your rest."

Sam rolled his eyes. "Do you have any idea how many times I haven't slept all night but still got to work and class the next day?"

She pointed at him. "That's not healthy and could be dangerous. You'll fall asleep at the wheel."

Hawkman chuckled. "It's okay, Sam. Appreciate your offer. But I don't think there will be any problems tonight. I'll be back before you leave for school. If not, take it easy and don't get a ticket."

Hawkman waited until dark before loading his rifle into the truck and checking under the seat for the night binoculars.

Jennifer walked out to the 4X4, concern written all over her face.

"Hey, what's the problem? Don't you trust your old man?" he asked laughing.

"You know that's not my concern. I just want to make sure you have your cell phone."

He pulled back his jeans jacket and showed her. "It's right where it should be. Hooked on my belt."

"I see you're carrying your Buck knife too?"

He nodded.

❖❖❖❖❖❖

Richard knew tonight would be his last chance to check Jerome's blade. It would be dangerous, but he had to know for himself. He didn't like the moonlit night. Not near as easy to sneak up on the shanty. The dog, of course, would be alert, so he'd make sure he had plenty of tidbits handy to keep the animal from giving him away.

He dressed in his dark clothes again, stuffing the plastic bag of goodies into the pocket of his sweatshirt. The knife, cell phone and flashlight were strapped to his waist. Taking a deep breath, he flipped out the house lights and started toward the back door when he suddenly stopped. Something flashed by the window. He glanced out and spotted headlights on the road some distance away. Standing rigid for several moments, he watched. The beams turned onto the logging road then suddenly went out.

"Who the hell is that?" he muttered. "Could it be Alberts? Maybe even Jerome coming home late." He grabbed his binoculars and tried to focus on the dark shadow meandering up the road. As it got closer, he could make out the outline by the light of the moon. He shifted and took a step nearer to the window. "Damn, that's Hawkman," he said aloud. "What's he doing up here this late and driving without lights?"

Richard slowly lowered the glasses to the table and fingered the strap. He doesn't trust me. But in his heart, he knew that wasn't the reason. Hawkman was worried about him and had every right to be. He took a deep breath and exhaled. I'm sorry, Hawkman, but I have to find out for myself."

Aware that the ex-spy would have all the paraphernalia for night time vision, Richard eased out the back door and headed for the small gorge. He figured Hawkman would park in that dense thicket of trees not far from the shanty, where he could see anyone coming or going.

The boy figured he could get within several hundred yards of the shack without being spotted if he took the back way through thick brush and gullies that sprinkled the landscape. It would take longer, but worth the effort if he could get there unseen.

Thrashing through the underbrush, Richard prayed that Jerome had drunk himself into oblivion and would be in a dead sleep. Discovering the empty liquor bottle he'd found in the the bushes to be the same brand he'd found in Jerome's trash can made him come to the conclusion that this man had visited his mother.

Also Richard vividly remembered how upset his mother had been after returning from Jerome's place. She'd walked up there one day shortly after his father died, bearing homemade jellies and jams to thank him for his kindness toward her ill husband. When she returned, she stormed into his room and told him never to go visit the hermit unless she accompanied him. She didn't explain why, only demanded that he give her that promise. Which he did, until that day he went to get carving instructions. Jerome never visited their place again while his mother was alive. Richard always wondered what she had seen or what this man had done to make her so angry.

He could see the outline of the unlit shack now. The closer he got, the more attentive he became on Midnight's whereabouts. Suddenly, it dawned on him that the hermit's truck was no-where in sight. The dog must be with him. Richard breathed a sigh of relief, yet kept the structure between him and Hawkman's hiding place. Slithering to the back side of the shanty, he looked into the window. His sight had adjusted well to the darkness, and he could see the bed was empty. Slipping around to the front, he tried the door. It opened with a slight twist of his wrist. He stepped inside, took the penlight from his waist and shined the thin beam around the walls inside. What he saw made him step back and gasp.

# CHAPTER TWENTY TWO

*Hawkman pushed up his eye-patch and peered through the* binoculars. He scanned the wooded area where he thought Richard would pass through to get to Jerome's place, but spotted no activity whatsoever. Had he missed the boy? His jaw tensed and quivered at the thought.

Kevin reported that Jerome and his dog left in the truck early this morning and had not returned by the time Hawkman took over the watch. Hopefully, the big man would be gone for a day or two. He certainly didn't relish the idea of having to face him.

Swinging the glasses around to the shack, Hawkman suddenly straightened. A movement at the corner of the building caught his eye. He brought the image closer into focus and hissed. "How'd that little fart get by me. I must be slipping."

No reason to get excited, he thought. Let the kid investigate. He's in no danger and might as well get this out of his system. The thought had no more swept through his mind, than he spotted the headlight beams of a vehicle turning onto the logging road. He quickly turned the binoculars in that direction. "Damn!" he said aloud. "It's the hermit."

He dropped the binoculars on the seat and started the 4X4. When he threw it into gear and pushed the accelerator, he realized something was amiss. He jumped out and couldn't believe his eyes. "Damn, how could I have done such a dumb stunt?" He'd backed into a huge fallen oak branch with a big sharp spur that had punctured his tire and locked itself under his fender. Kicking at the tire, he cursed under his breath. The thought of driving up behind Jerome to startle him and give Richard a chance to escape, just went down the drain. Now things could really get dangerous. He'd have to hoof it, which would take him at least fifteen minutes at a fast run. Would he have time? Not wasting any more precious seconds, he jumped back into the truck and put a quick call over the CB for back-up.

Slapping his hand against the Colt in his shoulder holster, he left the rifle in the truck, grabbed the flashlight and took off in a dead run.

✛·✛·✛·✛·✛

Richard eased the beam of his flashlight back onto the wall of the one-room shanty. A shiver ran through him when he remembered his mother's warning words, "Never go to the hermit's place without me." Now he understood why. The whole surface of the four walls were plastered with pornographic scenes involving not only nude women, but also children of all ages. Even though Richard's innocent eyes had never seen such trash, his stomach formed a knot and bitter bile invaded the back of his throat. Slowly he reached down to his belt and pulled his knife from the sheath.

✛·✛·✛·✛·✛

Alberts had just rolled through the fast food place in Yreka, picking up a midnight snack, when the dispatch message blasted over his radio. He glanced at his partner Jim Perkins, who rolled his eyes when he recognized the location.

"Tell 'em we're on our way," Alberts said, hitting the gas pedal and flipping on the siren. He knew it would take them over thirty minutes to reach the area, but his gut told him that if the one-eyed Jack was involved, this call would be centered around that deaf kid. He wouldn't miss the happenings out in that god forsaken country for nothin'.

"Keep an eye out for deer," Alberts instructed. I don't need hitting one of those animals at this speed."

Jim straightened and stared straight ahead while munching on his hamburger and fries.

Alberts wondered what the hell would be going on in that neck of the woods at this hour. It seemed odd that the message reported the emergency at the home of Jerome Arnold, the hermit. Maybe it didn't involve the deaf kid after all. Maybe the big man had had a heart attack.

Naw, that didn't fit. Why would Hawkman be there? He's the one who called in. Alberts smirked. So the one-eyed Jack can't cope by himself this time. Needs help, heh? Will he be surprised when he sees who's coming to his rescue. Then he frowned. Could be he's surrounded by a bunch of motorcycle thugs? Now, those types the deputy didn't like to deal with at all.

He glanced at his partner. "If we need back up, who else is on duty?"

"We're on a skeleton crew tonight," Jim said. "I think there's only two other cars patrolling."

Alberts hit the steering wheel with the palm of his hand. "Damn. Well, we better make sure we have everything handy."

Perkins shot him a sideways glance. "What do you mean? We have our guns and pepper spray. What else do we need?"

"We might need tear gas."

"Why? That call sounded like someone's stranded."

"Hawkman ain't stranded. If that had been the case, he'd have called his wife. There's something else going on up there and I want to be prepared. Just put a canister here in the front seat."

The young officer shrugged. "We don't normally carry it."

"Shit. What kind of cops take care of this area anyway?"

Perkins sighed. "Look, Alberts, this isn't Los Angeles. The chief never felt we needed tear gas in our county. The closest thing we've had to a riot is a bar-room brawl and it didn't warrant tear gas. We broke it up by just being there and threatening the group with pepper spray. Anyway, tear gas is usually brought in by the riot squad, and we don't have one of those either."

"Boy, this is some puny squad."

"Well, Alberts, if you don't like it, you know where the door is."

The deputy's eyes narrowed. "Watch your tongue, boy."

Jerome had been hired to clean out one of the rancher's barns and had been paid a flat fee in advance, but the owner told if he did an exceptional job he'd be paid an extra forty dollars. Jerome didn't mind the work, but what bothered him the most were the two little girls, who looked to be about four or five years old, playing in their playhouse near the structure where he was working. They happened to be playing dress up and would prance around in only their panties as they changed from one garb to another, causing the sweat to break out on his forehead. Their cute little bottoms and bare chests caused very uncomfortable changes in his own body. He had to avert his eyes and focus strongly on the job at hand.

He knew better than to stare, as the mother kept checking out the back door to see how the girls were doing. If she spotted him staring at the children, she'd run him off the property and his reputation would be ruined. Jerome knew he'd have to keep his sexual tendencies to areas far from home to avoid being caught.

To the relief of the hermit, the little girls were finally called inside and he hustled to scrape the last of the manure off the inside wall of the milking area. As darkness invaded the barn, he found himself working only by the light of the moon until the owner came down carrying a lantern.

"Hey, Jerome. You could finish tomorrow. You don't have to work all night."

"I've almost got 'er whipped. Just another hour or so, unless you want me to leave."

"No, you're not bothering us. I just figured you'd be mighty tired." The man held up the lantern and glanced around the barn. "Man, you've done a great job. You've got this place looking brand new." He dug into his pocket and pulled out the extra cash he'd promised. "You've earned every dime, Jerome. I'll certainly pass the good word to the other ranchers."

The hermit ducked his head. "Thank ya, sir. Appreciate it."

"I'll leave this light for you. Just turn it off and put it on the front porch of the house when you're through. Also, slide the barn doors shut."

"Will do," Jerome said, pocketing the bills as the owner walked out.

He worked for another hour and half, sweeping out the barn

and piling the residue on a large compost pile outside. Finally, Jerome wiped his hands down his filthy pants and put on his dirty coat. Carrying the lamp, he slid the big barn doors closed and called the dog. "Come on Midnight, let's go home."

Turning off the lantern's wick, he waited a few moments making sure the flame had died before setting it on the man's porch. Then he lumbered toward his truck. Midnight jumped into the back as Jerome squeezed his big frame under the steering wheel.

On the way home, his thoughts went to the little girls. His hand dropped between his legs and he unzipped his pants. As he approached his house, he'd swear he caught sight of a flash of light coming through one of the windows. Yes, there it was again. "Now, who the hell is messing around my place," he hissed.

Jerome tried pushing on the accelerator, but the old pick up just groaned and kept at a slow pace as it made its way up the hill. Cursing, the hermit kept one eye on the road and the other on his place. He slid his knife from the sheath on his belt and laid it on the seat.

⟨⊹⟩∗⟨⊹⟩∗⟨⊹⟩∗⟨⊹⟩

Richard started in the corner of the room, digging his knife into the wall near the ceiling, then slashing downward, peeling the lewd pictures off with one swipe. He let the pieces flutter to the floor as he moved along rapidly with his sharp blade, repeating the gesture until one wall had been stripped clean within minutes. Sweat ran down the sides of his face and broke out on his forehead. He wiped it off with the back of his hand as he stepped up on top of a wooden box, sitting next to Jerome's rickety old bed. It tilted and dumped its contents onto the floor. Richard shined the flashlight down on the objects that fell out. He didn't recognized anything he saw, but the sizes and shapes indicated they had something to do with the pictures on the wall. The idea made him nauseous.

Richard's thoughts went to his mother as he continued to rip at the wall's surfaces. She'd obviously discovered Jerome's hideous hobby. But then he remembered she said when she'd visited the man wasn't home. So more than likely she found the door unlocked as he did and came inside to leave the gifts. When Jerome came home and found them, he knew she'd seen the pictures. With his secret no longer safe, he came after her.

Jerome must have been in the area the day of her murder. The piece of paper he'd written the blade sizes for the carving were on the back of a receipt from the Copco Lake store, which was only open from ten in the morning until three in the afternoon. The receipt was dated June second, the day she died.

With all his might, Richard plunged the knife deep into the wall and tore out part of the old crumbling sheet rock, poking a hole to the outside. He glanced through the opening and his mouth went dry. Jerome's old truck had just turned onto the dirt driveway and was headed toward the shack.

◆❁◆❁◆❁◆❁◆❁◆

Even though the moonlight afforded some illumination, Hawkman fell to his knees twice after stepping into an animal hole as he raced across the field. He kept his eye on the headlights of Jerome's truck. Fortunately, it didn't have a lot of power and the climb up the hill to the shanty would take a few minutes. Hopefully, giving Hawkman time to make it to the shack before Jerome.

# CHAPTER TWENTY THREE

*Richard peered through the opening and his feet froze to the* spot. His heart pounded so hard that his chest hurt. The shanty had only one door and when he tried to open the lone window, he found it nailed shut. He had no other choice but to meet Jerome face to face within a matter of seconds.

He gripped his knife and wondered if he should throw it at the hermit the minute he came through the door. But what if he missed? Then he'd have no other means of defense. Richard figured he'd better hold on to the knife. At least he might be able to cut himself free of the man's grip, if he grabbed him.

The boy stepped back against the wall and held the knife tightly, hiding it behind his thigh out of sight. Sweat ran down his back, soaking his sweatshirt as he stared at the door.

Suddenly, it flew open. Richard jumped. A large silhouette filled the doorway and the glaring light from a flashlight blinded his view. After a few seconds, the brightness dropped from his face and a harsh glow filled the room from the lone bulb hanging on a cord in the center of the ceiling.

"What the hell are you. . .?" Jerome tossed the flashlight onto the bed, his gaze drifting around the room. Then his eyes narrowed and he met Richard's wide-eyed stare.

Slowly, the hermit brought up his knife and wagged it. "You bastard! Curiosity got the best of you, did it? Just like that pretty little mom of yours. Can't leave an old man and his nasty habits alone, can ya? Gotta find out what he does in his spare time?" Jerome took a step forward, his knife pointed at Richard's gut. A malicious grin spread across his mouth, saliva bubbling at the corners. "You had no right to come in here and destroy my wallpaper. You've invaded my privacy." He lunged forward, but Richard side-stepped and brought his own blade up in a threatening manner.

"Ah, ha!" Jerome laughed. "So we're about to have a duel between teacher and student?" His eyes glistened as he stared at the boy. "Whatsa matter? Cat got your tongue?"

"Why did you kill my mom?" Richard blurted, his insides trembling. "She didn't do you any harm."

The hermit glared at him. "You're too young to understand the desires of a man. Francine was beautiful. When your pappy got sick, I tried to show her I cared. But she didn't like me. Then one day she came here when I wasn't home and left gifts inside my house." He waved his free hand toward the walls. "She saw things that didn't please her, just like you."

Richard realized he'd backed himself into a corner with Jerome blocking his exit. He stiffened when the huge man moved toward him.

"Stay back," Richard said, pointing the knife at the hermit's belly.

Suddenly, Jerome's lips moved swiftly. Richard read them as yelling at the dog to shut-up. He prayed Midnight was barking at Hawkman and not at some varmint that had wandered into the yard.

⊹╴✦╴✦╴✦╴✦╴⊹

Hawkman's feet hit the hard-pan trail about the same time Jerome's truck crested the hill. He dropped to the ground and rolled into the gully alongside the road to avoid the headlight beams. Once the pick-up had turned into the yard, he bounded to his feet and ran hunched down beside the fence until he reached the back of the house. He heard the grinding brakes as Jerome brought the pick-up to a stop. Gun in hand, Hawkman crept around the side of the shanty, then started to turn the corner toward the front, but came to an abrupt halt. A snarling Midnight stood between him and the door. He holstered his gun, and eased his Buck knife from the sheath. If the animal came after him, he'd have to kill it.

A shaft of light shimmered through the partially closed door and Hawkman could hear Jerome's thick voice. He knew that Richard faced eminent danger. Hawkman also knew he had to be careful, as both the hermit and the boy had their knives unsheathed and were experts in hitting targets. It could be disastrous if he got in the way.

His back against the side of the shack, he inched his way toward the door, keeping an eye on the dog. The hackles on the animal's back were raised all the way to his tail and he could attack at any moment.

Jerome's gruff voice reverberated through the walls, commanding the dog to shut up. Hawkman breathed a sigh of relief when Midnight dropped his tail between his legs and scooted off under the porch. He immediately sheathed the knife and brought out his gun.

He stepped to the door and pushed it open. "Drop the knife, Jerome."

The sudden appearance of Hawkman distracted Richard, enough that he dropped his guard, which gave Jerome just enough time to grab the boy in a crushing hold and put his knife at his throat. "Tell the boy to drop the damn knife," the hermit hissed.

"Drop your knife, Richard," Hawkman ordered, never letting his gaze stray from Jerome's face. The boy's blade clattered to the wooden floor. Staring at Hawkman, Jerome pressed the knife against the flesh of Richard's neck, causing a small bead of blood to ooze across the blade. "I wouldn't do anything foolish if you want this boy alive. Drop your gun, put your hands above your head then move over against the wall."

Hawkman obeyed, throwing the gun onto the bed, then lifted his arms high as he stepped back. Jerome, clutching Richard to his chest, the knife still at his throat, dragged him toward the door. Hawkman mouthed, "Keep cool," as the boy brushed past him.

As soon as they were outside, Hawkman snatched his gun from the bunk. But when he looked out, he realized he couldn't get off a shot without putting Richard at risk. Jerome had turned around and was walking backwards so that Richard shielded him from Hawkman's bullets.

When the hermit got to the pick-up, with a firm grip on the boy's wrist, he quickly shoved him inside and scooted in beside him. At least, he'd removed the knife blade from Richard's throat. but still waved it in his hand. The pick-up's engine roared alive and Jerome drove off down the logging road.

Hawkman grabbed for his cell phone, but discovered it was gone. He must have lost it when he rolled into the drain area alongside the road. The wailing of a siren reached his ears and he prayed they'd stop the truck. But, of course, they wouldn't, he'd only called for an emergency back-up, never mentioning a murderer on the loose. He raced down the dirt road, hoping he'd meet the patrol car in time.

⊹⊱⊰⊹⊱⊰⊹

Alberts turned on the logging road toward Jerome's place, almost side-swiping the truck that barreled around the corner heading in the direction of Klamath Falls.

"Now, who the hell's drivin' around out here at this time of night?" Alberts yelled, hanging onto the steering wheel as the car swerved.

Jim twisted his neck and squinted at the pick-up. "Looks like that's hermit's old beat-up wagon."

"There's somethin' screwy goin' on here." Alberts hit the accelerator and started the climb up the hill.

"Hold it!" Jim yelled. "Someone's up ahead waving for us to stop.

Alberts came to a screeching halt and Hawkman jumped into the rear seat. When he saw the driver, he shook his head and mumbled, "This isn't my lucky day." He punched Alberts on the shoulder and pointed out the back window. "Follow that pick-up you just passed. Jerome's got Richard and he'll kill him if we don't get to him fast."

Alberts twisted the steering wheel and made a U-turn, sending a dust cloud that covered the view of the moon. "What the hell's going on?" he yelled over the sound of squealing tires and engine noise.

He sped down the road as Hawkman gave him a quick run

down of the events that had just occurred. "Jerome's crazy. He thinks if he shuts up the boy then no one will know he's a dirty old man with porno pictures plastering his walls." He didn't disclose to Alberts that he suspected Jerome killed Francine.

"What the hell was Richard doing at his place anyway? The kid like that kind of stuff?" Alberts smirked.

Hawkman glared at the back of the deputy's head with disgust. "Looking for Jerome's knife."

"That kid could never get it off Jerome's belt. I've heard the hermit even sleeps with it. And I hear he can whip a knife around faster than the eye can follow. Understand he learned it from the Indians."

"Yeah, and he taught Richard how to use one too. But the boy's knife is on the shanty floor, so he's weapon less right now. I'm afraid if we don't get to them fast, we'll find Richard all cut up."

Alberts gulped. "Oh God! I don't want to see that."

⋄⋄⋄⋄⋄⋄⋄

Richard kept his eyes on the huge man sitting beside him. He watched the sweat drip from the end of Jerome's bulbous nose onto his fat legs. Moonlight beams flickered off the the blade of the knife Jerome held in his left hand as he steered the unruly truck down the rough road. With his right hand, he gripped Richard's wrist so tight, that the boy felt he'd lost all feeling in his fingers.

"When the truck lurched around the corner, missing the police car by inches, Richard was thrown into the dashboard and slipped to the floor, preventing him from even seeing the car, much less attempting any signal for help.

Jerome yanked him back upon the seat. Richard stared at him with hatred. "Where are we going?"

"It won't matter," Jerome said, throwing his head back with hideous laughter.

"So what are you going to do? Slit my throat like you did to my mom and dog?"

"Hey, I wouldn't have killed your dog if your ma hadn't sicced him on me."

Repulsion welled in Richard's heart. If only he had his knife, that bastard would be dead right now.

"Why did you rip my mother's clothes?"

Jerome chuckled, showing his brown stained teeth through his parted lips and glanced at Richard. "Relax. She never knew about that. She'd already died."

Richard squeezed his eyes shut for a second and swallowed the lump in his throat. How he wished he'd listened to Sam and talked with Hawkman. Maybe if he had, he wouldn't be in this situation.

Suddenly, the hermit glanced into the rear view mirror and stiffened. Obscenities rolled out of his mouth and for just a split second, he released his grip on Richard's wrist. That's all it took. The boy whipped his arm free and threw open the passenger side door.

Startled at Richard's action, Jerome lost control of the truck. It veered toward the side embankment, hit a large rock, flipped over and showered sparks as it skidded across the stones. It finally came to rest on its side in the middle of the road.

# CHAPTER TWENTY FOUR

*Alberts slammed on the brakes. "Hold on!" The patrol car skidded* several yards, missing Jerome's pick-up by inches. Hawkman hadn't put on his seat belt and his body slammed against the door before the car came to a rocking stop.

He leaped out and raced to the front of Jerome's truck. Unable to see through the shattered windshield, he climbed up the side and yanked open the driver's side door.

"Bring me a flashlight," he yelled at Alberts. His heart beating fiercely, he grabbed the light from Alberts' hand and shone it around the interior of the wrecked truck. Jerome's blood covered body filled the cab and as hard as Hawkman tried, he couldn't get the dead weight of the man to shift one way or the other.

Scared that Richard was under Jerome, he scampered down from the truck. "We've got to upright this thing. Richard is bound to be under Jerome and could be crushed to death.

The three men heaved on the truck until they finally jolted it back up on its wheels. Hawkman jumped around to the passenger side and immediately noticed the door had been jammed open. Richard's body was nowhere in sight. Blood spewed from Jerome's wounds, his eyes were open and fixed. It appeared that the hermit's head had gone through the windshield as jagged pieces of glass hung from his face and neck.

"Alberts, get an ambulance out here," Hawkman ordered, before running down the road in the direction they'd come, searching the shoulder with the flashlight beam.

Jim Perkins ran along behind Hawkman, calling Richard's name. Hawkman finally stopped and took hold of the officer's shoulder. "Perkins, the kid's deaf. Just flash your light up and down the edge of the road.. If he's conscious, he'll make his presence known. Otherwise, keep your eyes open for a body."

The officer ducked his head. "I knew that. I just wasn't thinking."

Hawkman slapped him on the back. "Keep looking. The boy could be hurt bad."

Alberts' voice and flashlight ray cut through the darkness as he ran to catch up. "Perkins, get back there and stay with the body. I'll help look for the kid."

Hawkman suspected the sight of all that blood had gotten to Alberts and he'd rather hunt for Richard in the darkness than wait for the ambulance.

Even though it was a moonlit night, Hawkman couldn't make out any markings on the ground where Richard might have leaped from the truck. He felt the boy would have fewer injuries if he'd jumped and not been thrown out of the vehicle. He stood for a moment and listened. Hearing no unusual sounds in an abnormally quiet night, where even the owls had ceased to hoot, he proceeded down the middle of the road. A chill traveled down his spine as he pointed the beam toward the trees that lined the road.

❖❖❖❖❖❖

In the split second that Richard felt Jerome release his wrist, he flung open the truck door and bounded out, stumbling and rolling to the side of the road. He never looked back and certainly didn't hear the truck screech against the rocks and roll over. He ran hard and fast, deep into the woods, until he thought his chest would explode. Finally, he stopped behind a large oak tree and looked in all directions. When he felt safe, he leaned against the trunk, until his breathing returned to normal.

He probably should have run down the middle of the road, but he couldn't take the risk of Jerome turning the truck around and searching for him. Jerome could work like an ox, but he couldn't run. He carried too much weight.

Richard wanted to make sure he'd put a good distance between him and that hideous man. He had no doubt Jerome would slit his throat, just like he'd done to his mom, and leave him in the woods to bleed to death. Now, he knew for a fact who'd murdered his mother. Jerome could travel to the ends of the earth. It wouldn't matter. Richard vowed he'd find him.

He stood with his back against the tree for a long time, observing the shadows and jumping at every flutter of a leaf. The moon had moved some distance across the sky and Richard felt exhaustion take over. He slid down the trunk, curled into a ball at the foot of the tree and fell asleep.

⟨⊹⟩⊰⟨⊹⟩⊰⟨⊹⟩⊰⟨⊹⟩

Hawkman and Williams leaned on one of the patrol cars as they watched Jerome's body being examined.

The coroner finally stood and glanced at Williams. "Looks like this man's spinal cord was severed in the accident, causing instant death." He knelt back down and continued taking measurements, then finally instructed the paramedics to remove the body.

Williams puffed on his stogie and stared into space. "No sign of the boy?"

Hawkman removed a toothpick from his pocket and stuck it between his teeth. "None. We've searched all up and down this road. I think he jumped out. But I don't know where. If he doesn't realize that Jerome's dead, he'll be scared and probably hide out."

"You're sure he was in that truck?"

"Yep. Saw Jerome put him in there myself."

Williams pushed away from the vehicle and called two of the patrolmen. "See if you can't round up a few of the ranchers in the area to help us find Richard Clifford."

"On horseback or on foot?" asked one of the officers.

The detective scratched his side burn. "Both. In this rugged terrain, horses might be a wise way to go."

"I hate to ask," Hawkman said. "But could you drop me off up by Jerome's so I can get my truck?"

Williams raised a brow. "I wondered where that 4X4 was. What happened?"

"I'll tell you on the way."

The two men worked the big limb loose that had wedged under the back fender of Hawkman's truck and got the tire changed before daylight broke.

Hawkman climbed into his vehicle and started the engine. "I'm going to search deeper into those areas near the road. Richard will recognize my truck and hopefully come forward."

Williams waved and headed back toward the scene of the accident where he'd instructed the search party to meet. Before Hawkman pulled onto the road, he jumped out and searched the gully for his cell phone, which he figured he'd lost there. Sure enough, he found it unharmed. He wondered if Richard had his on him. It wouldn't hurt to give it a try. The sun had just started to peek over the hills when Hawkman keyed in Richard's number and stared at the face of the phone, praying it would tell him the message had been received.

⊹⊱⊰⊱⊰⊱⊰⊱⊹

Richard stirred on his bed of dead leaves and protruding roots. His eyes flew open when he felt a strange sensation centered at his waist. He automatically swatted the area, thinking some bug or lizard had slipped under his sweatshirt. Then it dawned on him that the cell phone, still attached to his belt had vibrated against his skin. He yanked it off, blinking several times as he stared at it. When he recognized Hawkman's number, excitement filled his chest. He dialed the number and counted to eleven.

He spoke softly into the phone. "Hawkman, I'm safe. I don't know where Jerome is, but he's the one who killed my mom. He wants to slit my throat too, but I'm hiding in the woods where he can't find me. Get the police to arrest him fast. There's a liquor bottle in my room in the closet. I know it has his fingerprints on it. Go get it. Also there's a receipt from the Copco Lake Store on the kitchen table that shows he was in the area at the time. It's all the proof you need. I'll keep in touch."

⊹⊱⊰⊱⊰⊱⊰⊱⊹

Hawkman yelled into the phone, "Richard, it's okay. You can come home. Jerome is dead!" When the screen went blank, he banged the steering wheel in frustration. How could he reach him? What kind of a code could he send that the boy might understand. Where was he?

He threw the truck into gear and jammed his boot down hard on the accelerator.

# CHAPTER TWENTY FIVE

*Hawkman's truck spewed a cloud of dust across the yard as he* came to a grinding halt in front of Jerome's shanty. Midnight scooted out from underneath the porch baring his teeth, his shackles straight up.

"I don't have time to fool with you, Midnight. Shut up and go lie down."

To his surprise, the dog tucked his tail and retreated back under the house.

Williams planned to search Richard's and Jerome's places today. He'd be here soon. Richard's knife lay on the floor inside and even though the boy might risk coming back for it, he'd best get it out of there now. Then he'd head for the Clifford place to get the bottle and note. Williams wouldn't realize their significance, so he'd better get them into a safe spot as soon as possible.

Hawkman hurried inside the shack, dropped to his hands and knees and shoved the trashy photos around until he finally discovered the knife half hidden under the bed. When he stood, he glanced at the walls and grimaced at the remaining pictures.

He dashed back to his truck and raced for Richard's. On his way, he keyed in his home number and warned Jennifer that a call might come in from the boy. If so, to let him know immediately. He gave her a quick run down of what had happened.

⋅⟨⋅⟩⋅⟨⋅⟩⋅⟨⋅⟩⋅

When the phone rang, Jennifer had just wiped off the counter after preparing a lunch for Sam to carry on his way back to school. Her hands wet, she punched up the speaker phone.

Sam, dragging a duffel bag, wandered into the kitchen from his bedroom. When he heard Hawkman's message, he dropped the bag, turned on his heel and dashed back to his room. He quickly pulled on his motorcycle boots and clumped out the door to the garage. Jennifer hurried after him.

"Where are you going?" she asked.

Sam tugged his helmet over his head. "I've got a few ideas of where Richard might be hiding."

Jennifer studied his face and knowing the determination Hawkman had instilled in their son over the years, it would do no good to argue with him. "This excursion better not take too long. You have a long drive ahead of you."

"Don't worry," he said, straddling the cycle.

"Let me get the cell phone." She hurried inside, then returned with the instrument which he clipped onto his belt. He then headed down the driveway and gave a quick wave as he turned onto the road.

Jennifer immediately went into the house and called Hawkman, telling him of Sam's scheme. "I only hope he doesn't get in the way."

"No," Hawkman said. "In fact, I think it's a great idea."

After hanging up, Jennifer stood staring at the phone for a few seconds, then sighed and headed for the computer.

⋅⊰❉⊱⋅⊰❉⊱⋅⊰❉⊱⋅

Hawkman looked in Richard's closet and found the bottle in the brown paper sack the boy had described, plus the piece of paper on the kitchen table. He dropped the receipt inside the sack and left the house. He slid the evidence under the cab seat and drove back to the site of the accident.

He parked at the side of the road and noted several men huddled around Detective Williams, some mounted on their steeds, others stood holding their horses' reins. They all looked up and Zanker's stallion shied when Sam roared up on his motorcycle.

Leading his mount, Zanker met Hawkman half way. "Do you think the boy's been hurt?"

"I reached him on the cell phone and got the impression he's fine. Of course, I had no way of telling him about Jerome's death. He's scared and running for his life."

Zanker nodded toward Sam. "So, what's your boy doing here?"

Hawkman pointed toward the hills. "He knows some secluded places up there and is going to check them out. The rest of us will spread out in the nearby fields." He hooked his thumbs in his back jeans pockets and shook his head. "We can only guess where the boy might be hiding. And we should impress upon these volunteers that no amount of yelling Richard's name is going to help. We're just going to have to use our eyes."

Zanker rubbed his chin. "You know Clay Roberts has a blood hound that the police have used a few times."

Hawkman glanced at him with interest. "Never thought about a hound. Is Roberts here?"

"Yeah, and he has the dog with him."

"Don't think I've ever met him. Point him out," Hawkman headed toward the group at a fast pace.

Zanker introduced Hawkman to a gray-haired burly looking man in his mid-fifties. "Clay, Hawkman is interested in using your hound."

"Sure, no problem. Got him in the back of the truck."

"Is he pretty good?" Hawkman asked.

"Yeah, but I need something with the boy's scent on it. Like a piece of clothing that hasn't been washed."

"I can get that within minutes. He lives just up the road."

Hawkman hurried to his truck and made a U-turn, Sam headed for the foothills and the rest of the men mounted their horses and proceeded toward the fields.

When Hawkman reached Richard's house, he dashed inside, went straight to the boy's room, grabbed a shirt off the bed and raced back to his truck. Roberts and Zanker were waiting and watched the dog's reaction after Hawkman shoved the shirt in front of the hound's nose. The animal immediately dropped his head to the ground and Roberts led him along the road until the dog stopped and let out a howl. The owner released the leash from the dog's collar and the hound took off in a run across the field with Hawkman and Roberts in pursuit.

The dog led them to the tree where Richard had spent the night, then dashed past it and stopped short at a small stream. They coached the hound up and down both sides of the bank for several yards, but the dog seemed to have lost the scent.

"Damn!" Hawkman exclaimed. "That kid's too smart for his britches. He must have suspected that Jerome might use Midnight."

⟨⦙⧈⦙⧈⦙⧈⦙⧈⦙⟩

Sam bounced over the rough ground, heading for one of the four sites where he and Richard had stopped on occasion when riding in the hills. They were small caves that had been formed by erosion and usually hulled out by some animal. The cougars especially liked them.

He found no signs of Richard in the first two burrows and proceeded to the third. The sun shown brightly and sweat trickled from under his helmet down his neck and cheeks. He had to stop several times to wipe the salty perspiration from his eyes and eventually tied a bandana around his forehead. Fortunately, he'd brought two containers of water and a couple of energy bars, plus the lunch Jennifer had fixed. He spent a couple of minutes under a shade tree to down a sandwich and get his bearings.

The third and fourth dens were a bit more difficult to locate. Hopefully, he'd turned in the right direction. The cell phone wouldn't work inside the interior hills, so he'd try again later.

After backtracking several times, he recognized familiar territory and finally found the third cave. But he didn't venture too close. A bear had taken over this den and he wanted no confrontation with that animal.

He swung away and hung a right over the rough terrain. One last place remained and he prayed Richard would be there. It seemed the most logical thing for the boy to do: hide in one of these lairs, far from his most dangerous predator, man.

As he climbed a small hill and came over the crest, his heart dropped. There were no signs of Richard. He stopped in front of the cave and peered into the vacant dark hole. He took off his helmet and wiped his sweaty face, then took a big gulp of water. Suddenly, he heard whistling in the distance. He glanced around thinking the heat had caused ringing in his ears. But no, he distinctly heard someone whistling.

Then he remembered the story Hawkman told him about how Richard had learned to whistle. He got off the bike, tilted his head and listened, trying to focus on the direction of the sound. Sometimes the hills played tricks with echoes. He stood for several seconds then searched the area with his eyes, but saw no sign of another human being.

He walked around on the top of the hill until the whistling seemed louder. Glancing down, he gave a yelp of joy when he spotted Richard on a small ledge below. He grabbed a small nylon rope he carried in the cycle's side bag and tied it securely around a boulder. Holding on to the other end, he carefully made his way down the steep incline. When he reached the boy, he stretched out his arm.

Richard grasped Sam's hand. "I thought I would die here."

"What happened?" Sam asked, wrapping his arm around Richard's back as they climbed toward the top.

"I think I sprained my ankle when I jumped out of the truck, and the long walk hasn't helped." He pointed to a slick looking boulder sitting on the outside of the cave opening. "I stood on top of that rock to check the cave when my ankle just gave way and I slipped over the side. It hurts like hell."

Sam had Richard sit on a rock while he rolled up the rope. He then gave him water and an energy bar. After inspecting Richard's puffy ankle, he shook his head. "Sure doesn't look good. You think you can ride on the back of the bike without it hurting too much."

Richard looked at him with fear in his eyes. "Jerome will kill us both if he spots us."

"Relax, Richard. Jerome's dead." He quickly related the story of the wreck.

The boy's shoulder's immediately relaxed and a smile formed on his lips. "Let's go."

An hour later, they roared down Ager Beswick and stopped at Hawkman's truck. The men searching the fields spotted the cycle with the two boys and started toward the road. There was much back slapping and loud greetings.

Hawkman knelt down and examined Richard's ankle. "We better get you to a doctor. It could be broken."

At that moment, Alberts walked up to Hawkman and pointed at Richard. "I've been instructed to bring this boy in for the murder of his mother."

Fear showed in Richard's eyes as he stared at the deputy.

Hawkman spun around. "Like hell you will!"

Alberts stepped back at the fire in Hawkman's expression. "Hey, I'm only obeying orders"

Hawkman's gaze searched the group of men. "Where's Williams?"

"He had to get back to the station and left me in charge."

Hawkman yanked his cell phone from his belt. "We'll see about that." He punched in Detective Williams' number and moved away from Alberts. "Williams, what the devil's going on? Alberts is talking about arresting Richard."

The detective's voice boomed over the phone. "For God's sake, can't that man get anything straight? I want the boy brought in for questioning. I didn't say anything about arresting him."

Hawkman shot a menacing glare at Alberts, who'd turned his back.

"I've searched the boy's place and found nothing. So where are those so called clues that you told me about?" Williams asked.

"I've got them," Hawkman said. "I didn't want them lost in the shuffle."

"I also need the boy's knife."

"I have it with me. Did you send Jerome's blade to the lab?"

"Yeah, but at this moment, we're no closer to the murderer than we were three days ago. Jerome's dead and the kid ran away."

"Look, Williams, we've found Richard, but you know he ran because he thought Jerome would slit his throat. You and I know he didn't kill and rape his mother."

"It's happened before. The DNA testing will prove that one way or the other. But I need to question him."

"I'll bring him in. But first, I'm taking him to the hospital to have his ankle checked. Looks like it could be broken."

A brief silence, then Williams spoke. "Okay, have Alberts contact me."

Hawkman went straight to the deputy. "Williams wants you to call him."

Alberts eyes narrowed as he stared at Hawkman, then he turned on his heel and headed for the patrol car. Within a few minutes, he called to his partner and they left the scene, the tires kicking up dust and gravel as the patrol car pulled away.

Sam watched them leave, then strolled over to Hawkman. "He sure seemed in a huff."

Hawkman scooted his hat back on his head and wiped his forehead with the back of his arm. "He's pissed because I won't let him be alone with Richard for any period of time."

"Obviously, you don't trust him."

"I don't." Hawkman then changed the subject. "You need to start back to school before it gets too late. I'm glad you found Richard. I'll take it from here."

Sam nodded and checked his watch. "You're right." He walked over to Richard and put out his hand. "See ya in about three months."

"Yeah, I know. Your next break."

With that, Sam climbed on the motorcycle and rode toward home.

⊹⊱⊰⊱⊰⊱⊰⊹

Alberts gripped the steering wheel until his knuckles turned white. His foot heavy on the accelerator, he sped down Ager Beswick toward Yreka.

"Hey, slow down," Perkins yelled. "You'll get us killed if a deer jumps out onto the road."

The deputy shot a blank look at him as if he'd forgotten the man was in the car. "Yeah, you're right," he muttered through gritted teeth, lifting his foot off the gas.

"What's eatin' you anyway?"

"That damned private one-eyed Jack. He's always interfering."

Perkins shrugged. "Just made life a little easier on us. We don't have to take that kid in."

Before Alberts had time to respond, a call came in over the radio. A bank robbery was in process at the First National Bank in Yreka and all cars were being called in.

"Holy shit!" Perkins said, sitting up straight.

Alberts threw on the siren and plowed down on the gas pedal in earnest.

# CHAPTER TWENTY SIX

*Hawkman helped Richard to the truck and opened the door.* "We'll get that ankle checked before going to the police station. Detective Williams needs your explanation about the evidence you found." he said, pulling the sack out from under the seat. "Also, he wants your knife."

Richard winced as he applied his weight on the sore foot climbing into the cab. "I don't have it. It's on the floor of Jerome's shack."

Hawkman reached into his glove compartment and handed him the blade. "I went by and found it."

"Thanks."

They rode in silence until they reached Yreka and Hawkman started down the main street toward the hospital. Cars were backed up for several blocks.

Richard turned toward him. "What's going on?"

Hawkman shook his head. "Don't know. I've never seen a traffic jam in this town."

Richard pointed to the officer walking down the lane, stopping at each car. When he approached the truck, Hawkman poked his head out. "What's happened?"

"Robbery in progress at the bank. The center of town is cordoned off."

"Can I get to the hospital?" Hawkman asked.

The policeman glanced at Richard's swollen ankle propped upon the seat, then spoke into his walkie-talkie and waved Hawkman through the traffic.

They'd no more stepped inside the emergency room, than the ambulance crew banged through the swinging doors with a gurney. Hawkman had to yank Richard out of the way to keep him from getting hit.

"That's Alberts," Richard said, wide eyed. "There's blood all over him."

Hawkman jerked his head around and noted the stained sheet covering the man. "Looks like he's been shot."

Moments later, Jim Perkins came racing through the door behind the paramedics. Hawkman watched him go to the injured man and whisper something into his ear, then stand back as the medical staff rushed the gurney towards surgery.

Meantime, Hawkman found Richard a seat and checked in with the receptionist. Perkins hadn't even noticed them yet and still stood staring down the hall. Hawkman walked over to him. "What happened?"

Startled, Perkins jumped, then wiped his hand across his face. "What are you doing here?"

"Getting Richard's ankle checked."

"Oh, that's right," he said nervously, glancing down the hall. "Alberts caught a bullet at the bank robbery. I don't know how bad, but he sure is bleeding a lot." Perkins stared at the floor. "I don't like the guy, but he's not bad, just cocky. He doesn't deserve to die."

Hawkman patted him on the shoulder. "Just because there's a lot of blood doesn't mean it's fatal."

He took a deep breath and let out a sigh. "I know."

Richard had his ankle x-rayed and no bones were broken, but he'd torn some ligaments. The doctor decided to put him in a walking cast to prevent more damage and allow the injury to heal.

Before leaving the hospital, Richard and Hawkman stopped by the nurse's desk and asked about Alberts. He was still in surgery and they had no word on his condition.

They left and headed for the police station. Just as they entered, two men were whisked through a rear door and hurried down a hall toward the booking area. Hawkman figured they were involved in the robbery. He guided Richard in the opposite direction toward Detective Williams's office and knocked lightly on the closed door.

"Come in," Williams called.

Richard turned in his knife and answered the detective's questions for over an hour, explaining how he'd found the empty liquor bottle under the bushes at his house and how he'd come by the receipt. Williams explained that probably neither of these items would hold up in court, due to the fact that Richard didn't turn them in the moment he found them.

"A good lawyer could tear all this apart. You could have easily acquired that bottle from Jerome's trash can. It would naturally have his fingerprints on it. The receipt could be anyone's, even though you tell me Jerome pulled the piece of paper out of his pocket. It's only your word. Never hold any evidence from the police, Richard. It could be to your detriment."

Tears rolled down the boy's cheeks as he clasped his hands tightly in his lap. "Jerome told me he killed her." His chin quivered. "And raped her after she died."

Williams shot a look at Hawkman who stood behind Richard. "When did he say this to you?"

"In the truck. He planned on killing me too. Maybe I should have let him, because you think I killed my mother." He wiped the tears away with the back of his arm and looked the detective in the eyes. "Detective Williams, I know it isn't right, but I was going to kill Jerome for taking away the most wonderful thing in my life, my mother. I loved her. She was all I had left after my dad died. Why would I harm her?"

Williams reached across the desk and took hold of the boy's arm. "I believe you, Richard. What I'm trying to say is you shouldn't have tried to take this task on by yourself. It could have cost you your life or you could have ended up in jail forever. Fortunately, we have tests nowadays that I'm sure will prove your innocence. And hopefully, I'll be able to relieve your mind within a few days."

On the way back to Richard's house, the boy remained silent for several miles, then he turned his eyes toward Hawkman and said in a very low voice. "I wish my Uncle Joe was here."

The comment gripped Hawkman's heart. He decided at that moment to try and do something about it.

The next day, Hawkman called Detective Williams. "How's Alberts doing?"

"He's going to be fine. Fortunately, the wound wasn't life-theatening."

"Thats good. Can he have visitors?"

"Oh yeah. He'll be out of there in a day or two." Williams cleared his throat. "How's Richard? I'm afraid the news he's still a suspect hit him hard."

"He's doing okay. But I think he feels a bit lonely."

After Hawkman hung up, he called the number he had for Joe Clifford. He expected an answering machine or a notice that the number was no longer in use, so it startled him to hear Joe's voice.

"Hello."

"Joe, this is Tom Casey."

"How's Richard?"

"Doing as well as can be expected under the circumstances." Hawkman quickly related the latest events. "He needs you here."

"You know I can't come back."

"I want you to level with me, Joe. How much do you owe Hal Jenkins, alias Frank Alberts?"

Joe sighed. "Five thousand dollars plus interest. Probably closer to six thousand now."

"Do you have anything saved to pay him back?"

"Yeah. I've been putting some money away."

"How much?"

"Close to five thousand."

Hawkman rubbed his chin. "Did you sign any paper that says you owe this money?"

"Yeah, I gave him an IOU. That's why he's after me, cause he thinks I ripped him off."

"If I could work something out, would you come home and be with Richard."

"Mr. Casey. I'd love to come home without fearing for my life or Richard's. But I'm not going to put that boy at risk anymore. He's had enough. And who knows what these tests are going to tell. What if they go against him?"

"If the boy's telling the truth, and I think he is, there won't be any problems. But he needs you here for more than those reasons. He needs his blood kin beside him. These are difficult times."

"I don't know, Mr. Casey. I could get killed."

"All Alberts wants is the money. I doubt he has murder on his mind. Let me see what I can do. Are you going to be home tonight?"

"Yeah, it's my day off."

"Okay. I'll call you back this evening."

Hawkman drove to the Yreka hospital. Alberts lay in bed reading the morning paper and glanced up when he entered the room.

"Hey, man, I'm a hero. Look at this article. Got myself shot and made the headlines."

Hawkman pulled up a chair next to the bed. "Yeah, congratulations."

Alberts put down the paper. "Guess that doesn't impress an ex-agent much, does it?"

"Hey, you're still alive and can enjoy the headlines."

"I can see you didn't come to give me a medal. What's on your mind?" Alberts asked, eyeing him warily.

"I want to know what it would take for you to leave Joe Clifford alone?"

Alberts laughed. "The money he owes me."

"You have a paper declaring the amount?"

"Yep, I sure as hell do. And the son-of-a-bitch is trying to squirm out of it by skipping."

"How much does he owe you?"

"What's it to ya, one-eye?"

Hawkman narrowed his gaze. "I want him back here with Richard. But he won't come because of you."

"So the kid told you where that bastard is. You just tell me and I'll get my money."

"Richard knows nothing. Just remember I'm the private eye. I found him, but I'm not telling you, so just shut up a minute and listen."

The deputy raised a hand in defeat. "Okay, okay."

"First of all, is there any other vendetta you have against Joe Clifford? Or is money the only thing you're interested in?"

"Just want my money."

"He owes you five thousand plus the interest. Is that right?"

Alberts raised a brow. "How the hell you find that out?"

"Doesn't matter. How much interest does he owe?"

"I ain't no loan institution, so the interest is high. I figure another thousand."

"Why did he borrow money from you anyway?"

"Gambling debt." Alberts grinned. "And Joe thought he'd make a killin' but he ain't got nothin' but the shirt on his back."

"That's why you used your birth name? So you couldn't be tracked as a police officer, participating in an illegal gambling game?"

The grin faded from Alberts' face. "So?"

"Look, Alberts, I want Joe Clifford here with Richard. I don't want to squeal, but I can't accomplish that if you keep him and Richard scared to death."

Alberts pointed a finger at him. "You get me five thousand dollars up front and I'll forget the damned interest and get the hell out of this hole. I hate this place."

Hawkman didn't expect this turn and jumped on it. "You serious? I thought you liked the area?"

"It's boring as hell. Yesterday was the most excitement I've seen for months. I'd leave in a heart beat and five thousand would get me outta here."

⟨⊹⟩⊱⊹⊰⊹⊰⊹⟨⊹⟩

Alberts watched Hawkman walk out the door. Could this private eye actually get him his money? Since Francine was no longer around, the fun had really dwindled. There sure weren't no pretty broads around here. Ya can't scoff at five thousand bucks handed to you. Hell no! It's enough to get out of this drag and to someplace new.

But, don't count your chickens before they're hatched, he remembered his maw saying. A lump formed in his throat when he thought of her. He closed his eyes and laid back on the pillow, wincing in pain from his shoulder wound.

# CHAPTER TWENTY SEVEN

*Hawkman left the hospital and drove straight to his office in* Medford. He didn't even take off his hat or jacket, but went straight to the phone.

He kept his fingers crossed that he'd catch Joe at home. His luck held.

"Joe, get a cashier's check made out to Frank Alberts in the sum of five thousand dollars and get it to me as soon as you can. Get an overnight carrier to bring it to my house."

"Are you sure he'll take just the five thousand?"

"I'm positive. Just talked to him. He wants to get out of the area."

"Oh, man! This is great news. But you gotta get that original IOU, cause I wrote it to Hal Jenkins."

"Don't worry. I'll take care of it. Then I want you to quit your job and high tail it back here by plane, boat or car. Richard needs you more than ever."

"I'll have to drive, won't have enough money left to fly."

"That's fine, just get your butt back here. By the time you arrive all this should be taken care of and you can move in with Richard."

"Man, it sounds good," he sighed. "I can stop running."

"But I'm going to be watching you, Joe. You haven't been very reliable in the past. You've got to take the responsibility of helping Richard care for the place, plus hold down a job. Remember Zanker is Richard's guardian now and he can kick you off the property any time he feels the boy isn't being treated right."

"I've thought a lot about Richard, Mr. Casey and I'm ready to help him out. It's really bothered me to think how selfish I've been. I want to thank you for all you've done."

"Just get here as soon as possible. That will be thanks enough."

"Mr. Casey. Do you have to tell Richard I'm coming? I mean, you think I could surprise him?"

Hawkman was taken back by the request, but liked the idea. "Sure, but keep in touch with me, so I know when you'll be here."

"Will do."

After taking care of some neglected business, Hawkman headed home. He thought about the excitement he'd heard in Joe's voice and hoped it was genuine. Richard didn't need any more heartache. But right now he needed his uncle, regardless of his reliability.

Jennifer sat at her computer engrossed in writing and glanced up when Hawkman walked in the front door.

"Hi. How's the Richard case going?"

Hawkman shook his head. "Hate to say it, but I'm still not sure whether he'll be arrested for the murder of his mother."

She looked at him with fear in her eyes. "Don't say that. You know he isn't guilty."

He nodded. "We're waiting for the test results. But Richard's clues are useless because he waited too long to turn them in. There is only his word to go on now that Jerome is dead."

Jennifer left her computer and went into the kitchen where she poured a glass of water. "When will the tests results be here?"

"They can get the DNA results back pretty fast now, usually within days. I'm expecting something by tomorrow. Williams has Richard's knife too, so they'll be running tests on it."

Jennifer hugged herself. "This has been a horrible ordeal for that boy. I'll be glad when it's over. I wish that uncle of his would return. Richard must feel terribly alone."

Hawkman went into the living room and sat down on the hearth. Jennifer followed.

"Well, I do have some good news." He related the events of the day and the possibility of Joe coming home within the week. "I think Frank Alberts will leave the area once he's gotten his money. And Joe won't have to worry about Frank's threats anymore."

"That's a relief. Does Richard know?"

"No, Joe wants to surprise him. I think that's a good idea. Then if he doesn't show, the boy won't be disappointed."

"You've got a point. Richard didn't draw a very dependable picture of his uncle."

Hawkman stood and scratched his chin. "I wonder what's happened to Midnight, Jerome's dog? I'm sure the animal won't starve, he's a hunter. But it's a shame to leave him alone. He's used to human companionship, even though it wasn't the greatest."

Jennifer's eyes lit up. "What about Mr. Harrington? He lost his wife a month ago and is all alone. He's a sweet old fellow and it might be good for him to think about something else besides his loss."

"Good idea. I'll drop by his place tomorrow and see if he's interested in taking in a lonely dog."

⊹⊱⊰⊹⊱⊰⊹

The next morning, as Hawkman got ready to leave, he asked Jennifer, "Are you going to be home this morning?"

"Yes, I'm working on a story."

"Good, the check might come from Joe. but I really don't expect it until tomorrow."

"No problem. I'll be here."

He stopped by Harrington's place and talked with the old man about the dog, but didn't tell him the whole story. "Jerome, the hermit, was killed in a car accident a couple of days ago and left a dog. Wondered if you might be interested in taking the animal in? As far as we know, Jerome has no relatives."

The old fellow rubbed the at least two day stubble on his chin. "Never thought about taking in a dog. But, might not be a bad idea since I'm alone now. Tell you what. I'll give it a try for a week or so. If it doesn't work out, I'll give you a call."

"Fair enough," Hawkman said.

"What's the animal's name?"

"Midnight."

Harrington nodded. "Bring him over and I'll see how we get along."

The old man shuffled out to the truck with Hawkman. "On

second thought, maybe I ought to go with you and see if the dog takes to me."

"That's a great idea," Hawkman said. "Grab some hot dogs or meat scraps if you happen to have any in the house."

Hawkman saw excitement light up in the old man's eyes. Midnight, don't blow this chance you've got, he thought, remembering how the dog bristled at him earlier.

As they rode toward Jerome's, Harrington did most of the talking. "This will be something new in an old man's life. Sounds strange doesn't it? But, I've never had a pet, even as a kid. Worked around animals all my life, just never got attached to any of them."

"I think you and Midnight will get along real well. I'm just hoping he's still around." Hawkman thought about all the police activity around Jerome's place. The dog could have disappeared.

After turning onto the logging road, Hawkman pointed to Richard's place. "Did you know the Clifford's?"

"No, never met them. But read about the woman's murder in the paper. Have they found the killer?"

"Not yet. Mind if I swing in for a minute and check on the boy?"

"Sure. I'd like to meet him. I understand he's a suspect."

Hawkman shot a look at the old man. "Who told you that?"

"Jerome, the hermit. I'd run into him at the Copco Lake Store about twice a week. We'd sit out on the porch and spit tobacco for half hour or so. After they found the woman's body, he told me he figured the boy had done it because he knew how to use a knife. I found it hard to believe a boy would kill his mother." He shrugged. "But, I guess it's happened."

Hawkman parked in front of Richard's house and turned to Mr. Harrington. "The boy is deaf. So when talking to him, make sure he can see your face. I think once you've met him you'll see what a lie Jerome fed you." Hawkman climbed out of the truck, only to be met by a tail wagging Midnight running around Richard as he limped toward the 4X4 in his walking cast.

Hawkman pointed at the dog. "What's Midnight doing here?"

Richard shrugged. "I couldn't leave him up there at that shack all by himself. So I walked up there, put a leash on him and brought him home. I left him tied for one night, then let him loose this morning. He didn't take off. Seems like he knows his master's gone."

"How's the ankle?"

"Fine. But this thing's a nuisance and makes my leg itch underneath."

Hawkman laughed. "Richard this is Mr. Harrington. He's interested in making a home for Midnight."

The boy's eyes clouded. "Oh."

"But, son, if you want that dog, I won't take him," Harrington immediately intervened.

"I'd like to keep him," Richard said, his eyes downcast.

"Well, then you shall," Harrington said. "I don't need a dog to take care of. I was just going to take him as a good deed."

Midnight had made his rounds of checking out both Hawkman and Harrington, showing no signs of aggressive behavior.

"That dog sure acts different when he's not around Jerome," Hawkman said.

"Midnight's a good animal. Jerome was mean to him," Richard patted the dog on the head. "He just needs loving care and he'll make a great companion."

"I believe that," Harrington said, calling the dog.

Midnight ran to him, tail a wagging and licked his hand. Harrington knelt and gave the dog the treats he'd brought.

⊹⊱⊹⊱⊹⊱⊹⊱⊹

On the way home, Harrington remained quiet, thinking about the gruesome murder. Could that boy have actually killed his mother and dog? Hard to say what kids think anymore. But what would be his motive? He's deaf and now alone. And he couldn't be much over seventeen, even though he looks older.

Hawkman finally broke the silence. "Sorry about bringing you all the way out here, Mr. Harrington. I had no idea that Richard would be interested in that dog."

The old man jerked his head around. "No problem. I enjoyed the ride and meeting the boy. I don't really need a dog to clutter up my place."

"Appreciate your offering though."

Harrington shifted in the seat. "Do you think he killed his mother?"

"No."

"Why is he a suspect?"

"He found her. No witnesses and no clues."

"Oh my God. That boy could go to prison for a crime he didn't commit."

Hawkman nodded, his jaw taut.

# CHAPTER TWENTY EIGHT

*Hawkman dropped Harrington at his house, then stopped by his* own place to check for messages.

Jennifer glanced up from the computer and smiled. "Nothing and no letter from Uncle Joe. So how did it go with the dog?"

He told her about the morning events, then went to the phone. Unable to reach Detective Williams, he left his name. He sighed, walked over to the sliding glass doors, gazed out over the lake for a moment, then stepped out onto the deck and into the aviary to check on Pretty Girl. When he went back inside, he stopped at Jennifer's desk and stared at the monitor screen. "I need to get Pretty Girl out again, but I've got too much on my mind. Think I'll go to the office, but will stop on my way and see if I can catch Williams. The reports should start trickling in."

She sat back and eyed her husband. "You're worried aren't you?"

He nodded. "Yeah. It bothers me that we haven't come up with any concrete evidence against Jerome. The DNA is really our only hope, unless his knife turns out to have the nick that showed up on the report. Unfortunately, that's going to be hard to prove. Even Alberts is still under suspicion. But Williams said he turned in a report that pretty well covers his ass. He has witnesses that will prove he wasn't anywhere near the area the day Francine was murdered. So that rules him out. If something doesn't show up to clear Richard, we may be in for a long legal battle."

Just as Hawkman opened the door to leave, the phone rang. He turned and came back to answer it.

"Hello."

"Mr. Casey, Harrington here. I'm calling because I can't get that kid off my mind. Not sure if this information will help or if it's important at all."

"I'm listening."

"I saved the newspaper that covered Francine Clifford's death. Her murder occurred on June second, right?"

"Yes."

"I've heard gossip around the lake that Jerome and the police deputy Alberts were both under suspicion. But that no one knows for sure if Jerome was in the area. Well, I know for a fact that he stopped at the Copco store that morning."

"Are you sure about the date?"

"Positive. Because Jake, the store owner, had offered to pick up a prescription for me when he went into town the day before. Told me to come by on the second, which I did right at ten o'clock when they opened. Jake and I were shooting the bull when the hermit walked in."

Hawkman's attention piqued, he quickly took a pencil and scribbled some notes on a pad. "Did you talk to him?"

"No, because he appeared to be in a foul mood and went straight to the bathroom. He came out swinging his hands and slinging water all over the place. He yelled at Jake for running out of paper towels. After he left, Jake went into the bathroom to replace them and called me. When I went to the door, he pointed at the sink and asked me what I thought the stuff on the basin looked like. I'll swear it looked like blood. We never thought much about it, 'cause he could have cut himself and wanted to wash it off. But now, the thought gives me the willies."

"Mr. Harrington, would you be willing to testify to that in court, if it ever got to that?"

"I sure would and Jake would back me up."

"Keep this information to yourself. I really appreciate the call."

Hawkman hung up and hurried toward the door.

"Wait," Jennifer called. "Who was that?"

"Harrington. First positive break we've had. I'll tell you later. Got to find Williams."

When Hawkman appeared at the detective's office, Williams glanced up with a solemn expression and motioned toward a chair. "Come on in. Just got the report on Richard's knife."

Hawkman pulled the chair up to the desk. "And?"

"The knife has been honed so much, they couldn't tell if there had been a nick or not."

"What about Jerome's blade?"

"Don't know yet. I expect that report, plus the DNA, within the next forty-eight hours."

Hawkman rubbed his hand across his chin. "I feel like it's hurry up and wait."

"Yeah, tell me."

"So what are your plans about the boy? Do you still feel there's enough evidence to arrest him?"

"I'm not doing anything until I get the reports. If they don't match up, that's when I'll be arresting Richard Clifford."

Hawkman stared deep into Williams gray eyes. "You know that boy didn't kill his mother."

"I don't know that for sure." Williams stood and walked across the room, his back to Hawkman. Staring out the window, the detective rocked back on his heels. "Sons have been known to kill and rape their mothers. I can show you files from across the country. Despite your training, you've let your emotions get in the way. What happened, Hawkman? Is it because he's deaf?" He turned and stared at him.

Hawkman slapped his hands on the chair arms and stood. "You might be right. But I believe Richard even if no one else does. And if it takes a lie detector test to convince people, we may have to go that route."

Williams pulled a stogie out of his pocket and headed for the door. "I'll let you know as soon as I hear anything."

❖❘❖❘❖❘❖❘❖

Richard limped around the yard with Midnight at his heels. He checked the chicken coop, then meandered toward the barn where Whitey stood on the other side of the fence, tossing his head up and down. Fortunately, Richard had put an apple in his pocket before leaving the kitchen.

He got to the fence, but found it too awkward to climb with the cast. Opening the gate, he went to the horse, rubbed his neck and fingered his mane. Whitey voluntarily got down on his knees for Richard to mount, but the boy patted the horse's chest, the signal to come back up on his hooves. "Can't ride you until I get this silly cast off," he said aloud.

Instead, he put his arms around the big animal's neck and hugged him, making sure the horse could smell the apple in his pocket. Whitey nudged the area and Richard laughed. "Can't fool you, can I?" He pulled the fruit out and took a big bite first, then let the horse have the rest.

Betsy the cow strolled up, wanting her share of attention. Richard checked her over for sores or any other problems that could arise from being out in the field. He found both animals in good shape. He wondered if Betsy was too old to have another calf. He sure missed the milk. He'd talk to Zanker, as he'd have to borrow his bull.

Slumping his shoulders, he leaned against the horse. That is, if he didn't get arrested. It made his heart ache to think anyone would even consider he'd hurt his mother. Why didn't they believe him? Telling them what Jerome said didn't seem to be enough. It appeared the world was against him.

Lifting his head, he saw a cloud of dust from a vehicle heading his way. He hurried toward the house and his spirits rose when he recognized Hawkman's truck. Hobbling toward the driveway, with Midnight still at his heels, he smiled when he saw Pretty Girl perched in the cab, her wings flapping when the vehicle rolled to a stop.

Hawkman poked his head out the window. "I'm taking her to hunt. Want to come?"

"Sure!" Richard said, climbing awkwardly into the truck, helping the stiff leg in with his hands. Before shutting the door, he pointed at Midnight. "You stay. I'll be back shortly."

They made their way to the knoll and Hawkman let the boy carry the falcon on his arm. He successfully got the bird to fly and the two men leaned against the truck waiting for her return.

Richard drew circles in the dust on the truck fender, then looked up at Hawkman. "Have you heard anything?"

"Only on your knife. They can't tell if it had a nick because you've sharpened it so much."

"There wasn't one. The blade's always been perfect." Richard let out a sigh. "But that's just my word and it's not good enough. No one seems to believe me."

Hawkman shot him a stern look. "That's not true. It's just hard for the law to be satisfied." He pushed away from the truck and stared into Richard's eyes. "If the DNA they found on your mother's body doesn't match that of Jerome's, they'll want a blood sample from you."

Richard's jaw went taut. He glared at Hawkman. "How could anyone think for one minute that I'd rape my own mother!"

Hawkman reached over and took the boy's arm. "Richard, I believe you. And so do a lot of other people. This will only prove it."

He yanked away from Hawkman's grasp and turned his back. Tears welled and he quickly wiped them away. "I wouldn't have the slightest idea of how to even go about it. I've never had a girl."

Turning around, he looked into Hawkman's face. "My mother was the most precious thing in the world to me. We were very close and I loved her with all my heart. Do you know how horrible it makes me feel to think they have to take a test to find out I didn't hurt her?"

Hawkman took a deep breath and exhaled. He couldn't even look the boy in the face. "It's for your protection, Richard. That's the only way I know how to explain it."

Silence reigned for several moments, then the boy looked up and pointed. "There's Pretty Girl."

Hawkman tossed him the glove. "See if she'll land on your arm. Remember how to whistle for her?"

"Yeah," he said, pulling on the glove and puckering his lips.

⊹∙⊹∙⊹∙⊹∙⊹∙⊹

The next day, the certified check from Joe Clifford arrived. Hawkman made a quick call to the hospital and found that Alberts had been released. He'd probably find him at his apartment and debated on whether to call or just drop by. Knowing Alberts, he decided it would be best for the deputy to see the check made out to him. The temptation of all that money in one lump sum would stop him from wanting that extra thousand in interest.

When he arrived at Albert's place, a black and white sat out front. Not wanting to expose the situation to anyone else, especially a police officer, Hawkman decided to come back later. He ran some errands and returned within an hour to find the patrol car gone. Strolling up to the door, he eyed the surrounding area. The neighborhood stood quiet with little activity outside.

He knocked on the door and shifted from foot to foot waiting for a response. Shortly, the door opened a few inches, and a sleepy looking Alberts poked out his head.

"Yeah. What'd you want?"

"I have something that I think you'll be very interested in."

"Can't it wait? I'm really tired and hurt like hell. I just got out of the hospital a few hours ago and have already had a bunch of visitors from the station. I need to get some rest."

"It's up to you. But I think this cashier's check I have made out in your name for five thousand dollars might make your rest a lot more comfortable."

Alberts raised his brows. "A check? Come on in, man!"

# CHAPTER TWENTY NINE

*It didn't take much talking for Hawkman to convince Alberts to* forget about the rest of the debt and take what he could get.

The deputy sat on the couch, his left arm hanging in a cloth sling. He leaned forward, his right hand supporting his elbow, as he stared at the check. "I see Joe had the fore-thought to make it out to Frank Alberts."

"That took a little convincing since the IOU was made out to Hal Jenkins. By the way, may I have that IOU please."

Alberts pushed himself off the couch and headed for the bedroom. He returned within a few seconds and handed Hawkman a crumbled piece of white paper. "I carried it with me for a couple of years, so it's pretty worn." He put a finger in the air and winked. "But still good."

"Would you mind signing it off?" Hawkman asked, holding out the note.

He carefully sat back down on the couch, scribbled his birth name and date then handed it back to Hawkman. "Well, you can tell Joe he won't be seeing me anymore. I'm outta here."

"I'm sure he won't shed any tears."

Alberts threw back his head and laughed. Then his expression turned solemn. "You know, private eye, that kid Richard ain't a bad boy. He can't hear and that might hinder him in his life. It liked to have drove me nuts while trying to court his mom with the both of them deaf. But they were good people. I hope nothin' happens to him."

"I'm sure Richard will appreciate your thoughts."

The deputy struggled to his feet holding his side. "I don't mean to be rude, but I've got to get me some rest if I want to get out of here in a day or two."

Hawkman shoved the IOU into his pocket. "Does Williams know you're leaving?"

"Not yet."

"Good luck on your next job." Hawkman started for the door. "I'll let myself out."

Relieved that things had gone smoothly, Hawkman breathed a sigh of relief as he climbed into his truck. He decided to swing by the police station and see if the test results had come.

Nodding at a few of the officers as he strolled down the hallway, he wondered how unhappy they'd be when they heard of Alberts leaving. He doubted they'd show much regret.

The detective's door stood open and Hawkman poked his head inside.

"Williams glanced up from a pile of paperwork. "Hey, Hawkman. Come on in. Always glad to see you. Gives me a chance to take a break."

Hawkman pulled up a chair and pushed back his hat with his finger. "Just thought I'd drop by and see if any test results have come in on the Clifford case."

Williams shook his head. "When they didn't show up today, I called. Turns out they had an equipment breakdown in the lab and had to send everything out. They put a rush on the tests, but that doesn't mean a damned thing."

Hawkman tried to suppress his disappointment. "Guess there's not much we can do but wait."

Williams leaned forward on his elbows. "How's the boy doing?"

"Got pretty upset when I told him you might need to draw blood. But it isn't the drawing of blood that bothers him. It's the idea that no one believes his story."

The detective nodded. "I can understand his frustration."

Hawkman slapped his hand down on the desk surface and stood. "I can see you're busy, I won't keep you. Let me know when you hear anything."

Williams gave a mock salute. "Will do."

⊹⊱•⊰⊹⊱•⊰⊹⊱•⊰⊹

Over the weekend, Hawkman spent as much time as possible with Richard, trying to keep him busy so he didn't have time to think about the problems at hand. But even when they took the falcon out, he sensed the boy's tension.

One of the afternoons, while waiting for Pretty Girl to return from hunting Richard blurted, "When are they going to arrest me?"

Hawkman took a sharp breath and skidded a rock across the hard packed ground. "Maybe never."

Richard stared at him, then picked up a rock and made it bounce three times farther than Hawkman's. He grinned. "Beat ya."

When Pretty Girl returned, they started back toward the house. Richard suddenly sat forward in the cab and pointed out the windshield at a cloud of dust some distance away. "Someone's coming."

Hawkman squinted, trying to make out the vehicle. "Wonder who it is?" The thought flashed through his mind that it could be Joe Clifford. But it had only been four days since he'd talked with him. Not time enough for a man to quit his job, pack up and split. However, it could be possible. He shot a look at Richard. Would the boy let his uncle have his mother's bedroom? That could prove painful. As far as he knew, Richard had not ventured into that room since her death.

They watched the car pass. "Who'd be going to Jerome's place?" Richard asked, his brows furrowed.

"That road continues on up into the hills. Maybe someone's sightseeing."

"You gotta have a four-wheel drive to go much farther than Jerome's. And that looked like a regular car," Richard said, his eyes following the vehicle.

"Beats me. By the way, who owns that piece of property?"

The boy shook his head. "I don't know. I thought it belonged to the hermit."

"Maybe Jerome did buy it and the mortgage company is going to put it up for sale."

Richard slid back in the seat with a downcast expression. "I wish I could buy it. But, I'm probably going to jail."

Hawkman shot him a look. "Quit talking like that. You're not going to prison."

Pretty Girl let out a squawk and spread her wings at Hawkman's stern tone. Richard jumped and let out a laugh as her wing feathers smacked him in the face. "What'd you say to make her do that?"

"Nothing in particular," Hawkman said, as he looked out the window on his side, his jaw taut at the thought of how long it was taking to get those damned tests back. This boy figured he'd be spending the rest of his life in jail for a horrendous crime he didn't commit. The whole scenario ate at Hawkman's insides. He tried to imagine how Richard felt.

After dropping the boy off at his house, Hawkman turned toward Jerome's shack to see if the vehicle they'd spotted had actually stopped or gone on by. Approaching the property, he saw the car parked out front and pulled in beside it. It had one of those magnetic signs plastered on the door that read "Miles Real Estate and Brokerage Firm." His intuition proved right. He strolled into the front yard where remnants of yellow tape still fluttered in the breeze. Suddenly, a slim woman backed out the front door of the shanty, her hand covered her mouth and her gaze was locked on the walls of the shack.

Hawkman cleared his throat. She almost jumped out of her skin, whirled around and let out a short scream. "Oh! You scared me to death." Her hand at her throat, she frowned. "Who are you?"

"Sorry, didn't mean to startle you. My name's Tom Casey, I'm a private investigator."

"Are you working on the Clifford case?"

"Yes. I saw your car go by while visiting my client."

She held out her hand. "Nice to meet you. I'm Loretta Miles."

"I wondered what they were going to do with this place. Is it going up for sale?"

She glanced inside the shack again and pulled the door shut. "Yes. But it should be burned to the ground. The man who lived here must have been demented. I certainly can't sell it in this condition."

Hawkman nodded. "Yeah, he was sick all right." She started back to her car and he walked beside her. "What's the asking price?"

She glanced back toward the shanty. "It has electricity, but it doesn't appear to have been wired to code. There's no running water. So about all we can hope for is getting the worth out of the land. Which I have to say isn't much." Pulling a card from her purse, she handed it to Hawkman. "Give me a call tomorrow. I should have something to tell you after I talk to Mr. Clifford."

Hawkman stopped in his tracks and stared at her. "Did you say Mr. Clifford?"

"Yes. Joe Clifford. I understand he'll be in the area within a day or two." With that she backed out and drove away.

Hawkman stood with his feet apart and his mouth open as his gaze followed the cloud of dust down the road."

# CHAPTER THIRTY

*The next morning, Hawkman headed straight for the County* Courthouse. He checked the parcel number he'd found on an old tax bill from Richard's papers and discovered there were two pieces of Clifford property side by side. The larger seven acre plot now belonged to Richard R. Clifford and the smaller three acre piece bordering it, belonged to Joseph David Clifford. From the dates it appeared that Joe and his brother Bob, had bought the ten acre plot together several years ago and divided it into two parcels. They had purchased the land for seven thousand dollars from the estate of a widow woman who'd passed away leaving no heirs.

Joe owned the property free and clear. Hawkman scratched his chin as he studied the paper. Why hadn't he mentioned it? Of course, why should he? It didn't affect Richard and it certainly wasn't any of Hawkman's business. The property wouldn't have brought in enough to pay off the gambling debt either.

He wondered if Joe knew that the hermit had taken up residence in the shack? Or had Jerome just found the place vacant and moved in. He could understand why Joe would put it up for sale. Why have that horrible memory haunting him and Richard every day.

According to the records, Zanker owned all the land surrounding the Clifford place. Hawkman wondered if Herb might be interested in purchasing that strip of rocky ground that wasn't good for anything but grazing. It certainly wouldn't hurt to inform him about the sale.

Knowing Herb Zanker, he'd bull doze that shack to the ground. Hawkman liked that idea and decided to talk to the rancher today.

❖❖❖❖❖❖❖

Joe jerked awake at the pounding on the top of his car. "Yeah, uh, what is it?" He rubbed a hand across his face and rolled the window down a few inches.

"You okay?" the officer asked.

"Oh, yeah," Joe said, finally coming awake. "Just needed some shut-eye. Been driving for several hours."

"At least you had the sense to pull into the rest stop. Some of these clowns think they're superhuman and can drive forever. Have a good day. Just wanted to make sure you were all right." He waved and walked away.

Joe checked his watch. He'd been asleep for five hours. The sun's rays were starting to breach the night and the stars had disappeared. He got out and went to the head. After washing his face, he returned to the car and rummaged through the the ice chest where he found a slice of baloney. Wrapping it in a piece of dry bread from the loaf he'd brought from home, he leaned against the car fender. He shook his thermos and discovered it empty, so he washed the meager meal down with a gulp of water. He'd grab a heartier meal up the road.

He thought about how surprised Richard would be when he pulled in, that is, if that private investigator hadn't told him. But Joe liked the authoritative tone of Casey's voice. And he'd helped him settle the score with Alberts. Yeah, he figured the private eye would keep his secret.

Excitement surged through him as he realized he could actually go home now and live in peace. He felt like a huge weight had been lifted from his shoulders. Now, if he could sell that piece of property, he'd have a little nest egg to get him and Richard started with a new life. He'd buy a special phone for the deaf, a television set, and then work on that little house. He smiled to himself. It sure made him feel good to think about these things. Getting back in the car, he checked the map and drove toward the northwest. It wouldn't be long now.

❖❖❖❖❖❖❖

Richard worked hard at the Snackenburg Stage Stop. It kept him from thinking about going to jail. The horse trainer had taught him how to care for these sleek beautiful animals. She'd commented to him on more than one occasion that he had a way with the steeds. When he entered the stables the horses showed no fear and always went right to him. She cautioned him never to frighten them or he'd lose their trust he'd instilled. Why would he do anything to scare these wonderful horses? He enjoyed brushing their coats and examining every inch of their lean firm bodies, looking for sores or bites from insects. Walking them in their individual pens, he'd watch for any sign of limping and examine their hooves daily for bad shoes. So far, he'd never been kicked.

Richard didn't look forward to going home to an empty house that held sad memories, so when his shift came to an end, he lingered a few minutes petting and soothing the beast. Then he slowly pulled on his motorcycle boots, gloves and helmet, climbed on his bike, putted out the driveway and turned up Ager Biswick Road. He rode at a leisurely pace until he approached his house and the low sun glinted off what looked like a car parked in front. Who could that be, he wondered and revved up the cycle. He didn't recognize the small light colored Toyota and fear crept into his heart mixed with a tinge of excitement at having a visitor.

No one occupied the car, so he drove straight to the barn and parked, shed his helmet and gloves then hurried toward the house, his eyes canvassing the area for the stranger. Even Midnight seemed unruffled and romped out from under the porch with a stick in his mouth ready to play. Suddenly, the smell of food hit his nostrils, something he hadn't smelled since the death of his mother. His heart squeezed at the memory. But how did a stranger get into his locked house? He rushed up the back rickety stairs and threw open the door.

Their eyes locked. "Hi, there guy. Thought you might be hungry after a long day's work. Hope you still like fried chicken as much as I do."

Richard bounded toward the man and they clung together in a bear hug for several minutes, tears streaming down their cheeks. Finally, Joe pushed Richard back at arms length and looked at him. "God, you've grown. You're a man now."

Wiping his face on the back of his arm, Richard grinned and nodded. "I'm so glad you're here. Are you going to stay for awhile?"

"You bet I am. Thanks to your private investigator, Mr. Casey, my problems are solved. I'm here for good."

Richard looked at him wide-eyed. "Hawkman knew you were coming?"

Joe furrowed his brow. "Who's Hawkman?"

"That's Mr. Casey's nickname," Richard said laughing.

"Oh!" He nodded. "Yeah, he knew. I asked him not to tell you. I wanted it to be a surprise. And, obviously, he kept his word. That's a good man."

Richard walked over and punched Joe's shoulder with his finger.

Joe looked at him curiously. "Why'd you do that?"

"Making sure I'm not dreaming."

After dinner, the two men cleaned up, then went into the living room and sat down. Richard became very quiet.

"What's on your mind, boy?" Joe asked.

Richard looked up at him, his eyes glistening. "I'm so glad you're here. But, you need a room. And the only other bedroom is mom's. I've only been in there a couple of times since she died."

Joe walked over and put an arm around Richard's shoulders. "You don't worry about that right now. I'll sleep on the couch. We'll take it slow and easy until you're ready."

✦✦✦✦✦✦✦

Hawkman left the Zanker ranch with uplifted spirits. Herb said he'd contact the real estate agency first thing in the morning. And without a word from him, Herb talked about getting a bulldozer out there as soon as possible to raze that shack down to the ground.

He decided to swing up and check on Richard before going home. Hawkman spotted the strange Toyota in front of the Clifford house soon after he turned onto the logging road. Uncle Joe came to mind immediately. Even though he hated to break in on a private reunion, he'd best make sure it was Joe Clifford. This case had taken on too many swings to take anything for granted.

The smell of food still lingered in the air when he knocked on the door. Richard, all smiles, yanked it open and grabbed Hawkman by the arm. "Come in and look who's here."

They sat in the living room for an hour talking before Hawkman brought up the question about the piece of property.

"I didn't realize you owned that parcel Jerome lived on until I spotted a real estate person up there the other day. Did he rent that from you?"

"No, I'd already left the state when the hermit came into the picture. Up until now, Jerome had never given anyone trouble. He talked my brother into letting him live in that shack. Bob felt sorry for him and strung a line of electricity up there from his box here at the house." Joe shook his head. "Little did we know."

Hawkman nodded and glanced at Richard, then back to Joe. "I understand you want to sell it."

"Yeah, I don't want the memories hanging over our heads. And it will give us a little nest egg to start our new life."

"Sounds like a good plan. And I think I've got a buyer."

"Really?" Joe asked, wide eyed. "That's great." He slapped Richard on the knee. "Your Mr. Casey's something else."

Richard smiled. "His name is Hawkman."

At that moment, Hawkman felt his cell phone vibrate against his hip and excused himself as he walked out on the front porch. After a few moments, his expression solemn, he poked his head back inside. "I've got to go. I'll talk to you guys tomorrow."

# CHAPTER THIRTY ONE

*His stomach tied in knots, Hawkman bore down on the* accelerator once he hit the paved road leading into Yreka. William's had only told him the reports were in. The detective's stand for justice made Hawkman nervous and made him recall the days when he served with the Agency. The rule of law had to be followed. Why should it be any different for Richard?

He wiped the back of his hand across his mouth. His gut told him the boy wasn't guilty, but what if these tests didn't prove his innocence? If Richard had killed his mother and dog, he was one of the cleverest murderers Hawkman had ever come across.

"The boy's too damn young and naive to have that kind of mind," he mumbled aloud. "No!" he exclaimed loudly, hitting his fist against the steering wheel. "He didn't do it. It had to be Jerome." He gripped the wheel with both hands. "Anyway that's what Richard has made me believe."

Hawkman hurried into the station and tried not to look over-anxious as he made his way down the hall toward Detective William's office. When he reached the doorway, he gripped the jamb. The office stood vacant. He took a deep breath and strolled back to the young receptionist whose desk faced the main entry.

"When is Detective Williams due back?"

She glanced at her blotter, then at him. "Are you Mr. Tom Casey?"

"Yes."

"He's been called out on an emergency, but should be back shortly and asked that you wait for him in his office."

Hawkman, his jaw taut, strolled back to the small cubicle. He tried to sit, but kept crossing his long legs. Staring at the detective's cluttered desk, he wondered what those top papers contained. Finally, he got up and paced. He stopped at the window and stared out over the parking lot, then checked his watch. What seemed like an hour had only been minutes. He pulled a toothpick from his shirt pocket and chewed on it vigoriously.

Suddenly, he heard noises in the hallway and recognized Williams' gruff voice giving orders. His stomach tightened even more when the detective charged into the office.

"Hawkman, good to see you. Sorry about the delay, but I got called out right after I phoned you." He motioned to the chair in front of his desk. "Sit, I've got good news."

Williams opened the file on his desk, drew out several sheets of paper and placed them in front of him. A big smile lit up his face. "Richard's been cleared."

Hawkman felt like a ton of weights had been lifted from his shoulders. "What were the results?"

"Jerome's DNA was all over Francine Clifford's body. They found his tissue and blood under her fingernails. There were marks on his neck and arms that indicated she'd really fought for her life. The dog had obviously attacked several times, as there were animal bites on his leg and arm."

Hawkman leaned back in the chair and sighed. "Thank God!"

"They still aren't sure when he raped her. The report indicates she was either dead or dying and wouldn't have realized what was happening." He handed the paper to Hawkman. "I'm not sure knowing that will give Richard any peace of mind or not."

Hawkman shook his head. "I don't know. But if he asks, I can at least explain." He glanced up from reading. "What about Jerome's knife?"

"The blade had been ground down with a grinder. It appears he got wind that we were looking for a nick. However, not only did the lab find Francine's blood in a small groove in the handle, but also the dog's. It had been washed off, but not good enough" He opened his desk drawer. "Speaking of knives. Here's Richard's. I'm sure he'd like to have it back."

Hawkman slid it into his jeans jacket pocket and the two men sat silently for a few moments. Putting the papers back on the detective's desk, Hawkman took a deep breath. "Jerome was a sick man."

"Yeah, we're getting reports from one of the neighboring counties about a ring of perverts they've broken up. Pictures are coming in of some of the members. I recognized Jerome in one of them, even though he had his hat pulled down over his eyes. You couldn't miss that big frame and coat."

"At least you don't have to deal with him anymore." Hawkman stood and put out his hand. "Thanks, Williams, for all you've done to help clear Richard."

The detective gripped his hand and stood. "I hope you understand I never wanted to believe that boy was guilty, but I've seen too many weird things happen not to press it to the end."

He nodded. "That's your job."

⊰⊱⊰⊱⊰⊱⊰⊱

Back in the truck, Hawkman called Jennifer on the cell phone, telling her he'd be late, but had good news. She urged him to tell her right then, but he refused, laughing. "Nope, you have to wait until I get home."

She met him at the front door and pulled him inside. He started by telling her about Uncle Joe's arrival and the good feeling he sensed seeing him and Richard together. He ended with Richard being cleared of the murder charges.

When he finished, Jennifer looked up at him with moist eyes. "I'm so relieved. But I knew this day would end happily."

"How's that?"

She pointed out the picture window toward the lake. "Ozzy was back on his branch this afternoon."

⊰⊱⊰⊱⊰⊱⊰⊱

Early that morning, Richard raked out the chicken coop and

checked each nest for broken shells. He'd be leaving for work soon and Uncle Joe was going into town to check with the real estate agent. Richard leaned on the rake a moment and gazed toward the direction of Jerome's shack. He couldn't actually see it because of the trees, but he still shuddered thinking about that horrible night. He thought it ironic that through all these years Jerome's place had belonged to his uncle and he didn't even know it. Of course, when the property was purchased, he was just a kid and could have cared less about what the adults were doing.

The thoughts brought back memories of his mom. He knew he had to get her room ready for Joe. She would have wanted it that way. And it wasn't fair to keep his uncle out on that hard couch when a perfectly good bed stood vacant. Richard realized he had to make that decision soon. But first, he needed to find out what the tests proved.

He sighed, leaned the rake against the chicken house and headed for the barn. Climbing into the loft, he dragged the large box that Uncle Joe had sent the guns in over to the attic hole and carefully dropped it to the floor of the barn. He'd saved this carton for a purpose and the time had come. He climbed down the ladder, dusted off the cardboard with an old towel he had hanging on a nail, then hoisted the awkward carton to his shoulder and carried it to the house.

Uncle Joe grinned as he came in the back door. "Need any help?"

"Naw, got it fine."

Joe followed him to his room. "I think your idea is a great one. Even though I hate to see you give it away. I'll be sure and pick up some wrapping paper for you while I'm in town."

"Thanks."

That afternoon, Richard found he didn't have any desire to linger around the stables. He wanted to get home and visit with his uncle. It felt nice having someone to go home to.

When he started up the logging road, he immediately recognized Hawkman's truck at the house. At least there were no black and whites. His heart pounded. Had he brought good news. He revved up the cycle and sped toward home.

He could hardly wait to get inside after parking his bike in the barn. Throwing off his helmet and gloves, he raced toward the house. He charged in the back door and found Hawkman, Jennifer and Uncle Joe sitting around the kitchen table. Glancing at their faces, he tried to read their expressions. But Hawkman didn't give him time.

"Richard, you've been cleared. Jerome killed your mother and dog."

Tears of relief slid down the boy's cheeks. He threw his arms around his uncle and they hugged for several moments. When they parted, Richard wiped his face with the back of his sleeve. "Hold on. I've got something for you."

Joe followed him into his bedroom. Richard gasped at the beautifully wrapped gift on his bed.

"I thought I better get this done just in case Hawkman would come by tonight." Joe mouthed to him.

"It's great! Help me carry it so I don't mess it up."

They carried the large decorated package into the living room, then called Hawkman and Jennifer in from the kitchen.

Beaming, Richard pointed to it. "This is for you for helping me."

Carefully unwrapping the large box, they pulled out a beautiful rug made from the hide of a mountain lion.

## THE END